A MATTER OF CHANCE

Julie Coffin

CHIVERS

British Library Cataloguing in Publication Data available

This Large Print edition published by AudioGO Ltd, Bath, 2012.
Published by arrangement with the Author.

U.K. Hardcover   ISBN   978 1 4458 7852 2
U.K. Softcover   ISBN   978 1 4458 7853 9

Printed and bound in Great Britain by
MPG Books Group Limited

CHAPTER ONE

One Monday morning, Emma Jones received a cheque in the post for fifty thousand pounds, left to her in her grandmother's will. It was to change her life for ever—but not in a way she ever could have imagined.

'Oh, Steve!' she said, laughing as he put his arms round her waist, swinging her off the ground while he kissed her. 'We can do so much now. No more falling over each other in this cramped little flat. We can afford the deposit on a house. New furniture. A better car. And a baby.'

He lowered her to the ground, his arms still holding her. 'It's only fifty thousand, Emma—not millions in the Lottery.'

'Only! Steve, it's a fortune.'

Picking up the slip of paper, he frowned slightly as he gazed at it. 'Then don't leave this lying around to get lost. Now that your bank has closed its local branch, you'd better pay it straight into my account today—in case we need to get at the money easily.'

Emma nodded happily. 'Yes, I will do. Now that we've got this, let's go house-hunting at the weekend, shall we, Steve?'

'Okay, if that's what you want, we'll go house-hunting,' he promised. 'But tonight we'll celebrate. How about Antonio's?'

She rested her cheek against his. 'Where you proposed to me? Mmm, very romantic. And expensive. But can we—?'

'Afford it?' He held out the cheque and grinned. 'Somehow I doubt there'll be any problem. Off you go, or you'll miss your bus. And don't forget to pay this in. It'll take a day or so to clear, and the bank will probably need you to sign something first, transferring it into my account.'

*   *   *

The restaurant overlooked the river and, gazing out through diamond-paned windows, Emma could see the soft glow of candles on their table reflected in the ripple of water.

Steve's eyes smiled at her, his long fingers curving round his glass of deep red wine as he lifted it in a toast.

'To a far better future,' he murmured.

'Our future,' she said, shivering a little at the sharpness of the wine.

Maybe she was a little drunk that night. She couldn't really remember. Everything was a delightful blur of enjoyment. And their lovemaking was intense. She'd never known Steve to be so passionate. But then, it was only three months since their marriage.

Three months. The most wonderful months of her whole life. And now, she thought, this legacy would make their life together even more perfect.

Her grandmother's married life had been long and contented. 'Perfect bliss,' she had frequently told Emma. 'And I hope that yours may be the same one day, my dear.'

Sadly Gran hadn't lived long enough to be at their register office wedding, but the wording in her will, making the bequest, read like a blessing.

To my beloved granddaughter Emma Louise, so that she may find everlasting happiness.

*   *   *

'You will be home this weekend, won't you, Steve?' Emma pleaded, as they ate their evening meal a day or so later. 'I hate it when you're called away so often.'

'You know that any time I spend away from you is agony, Emma, but I have to go where the problems are,' he said, leaning across the table to stroke her cheek. 'It's all part of being an insurance assessor, sweetheart.'

'Not this weekend. Please,' she begged.

His dark eyes narrowed as he smiled and linked his fingers with hers. 'Can't help it, love—if there's a hurricane, or torrential rain, or the rivers decide to burst their banks, then . . .'

She smiled triumphantly. 'No, they won't! The forecast is for sunshine.'

'So—it'll be a fire, then,' he laughed,

3

squeezing her hand.

The following day was Friday. Planning the weekend of house-hunting ahead of them, Emma decided to call in at Steve's bank. The cashier was a girl she'd been at school with, who smiled in greeting.

'Hi, Emma. Everything okay?'

'Fantastic, Jane! Steve and I are off viewing houses tomorrow. I've got my eye on one of those new ones over near the park. Could you just make sure that cheque I paid into his account has gone through all right? We may need to put down a deposit straight away, you see. They're being snapped up so quickly.'

'Well, it is his account and, officially, I'm not allowed to tell you, Emma. But now you're married, why don't you open a joint account here?'

Emma laughed. 'Oh, we'll get round to it eventually. Since the local branch of my bank closed, my own account has been moved to the main one in town, but it's not so easy to access there. Anyway, has the cheque been cleared? I'm sure you can tell me that.'

Jane tapped the keys of her computer. 'Yes, it was cleared yesterday,' she said slowly, her forehead creasing into a frown.

Noticing, Emma asked, 'Is something wrong?'

'Fifty thousand pounds was withdrawn from the account at nine thirty-eight am—just after the bank opened this morning.'

'But it can't have been. Steve would have told me if he was going to do that. You've made a mistake—pressed the wrong key or something.'

Jane spoke quietly. 'There's no mistake, Emma. Maybe you should contact Steve and . . .'

Without waiting to hear more, Emma turned and, pushing her way past a growing queue of customers, escaped through the heavy door.

There had to be some simple explanation. She needed to phone Steve. It was something he'd always told her not to do. He could be in the middle of a ruined building. Any distraction would be dangerous.

Flipping through her diary, she found the number, and pressed the keys on her mobile. Silence.

She tried again. Nothing.

Obviously, his mobile wasn't switched on. Oh, Steve, why now? she raged. If only she knew which company he was working for that day. Being freelance, he went wherever, and whenever, a job occurred. That's what he'd always told her.

Maybe his cash card had been stolen and someone else had used it, she thought. But fifty thousand pounds—could you get so much money from a cash machine? There must be a limit. And what about the pin number?

Even by travelling from one cash dispenser

to another, it would take days to make up fifty thousand. Besides, Jane had said it was withdrawn at nine thirty-eight that morning. That meant it had been done in one transaction.

It could only be Steve. Maybe he needed the money temporarily, Emma reasoned. Do insurance assessors pay out instantly to people who have lost their property? Surely not in cash, though?

Steve's job was to go to properties to check on claims made, work out that the value stated was correct, and report back to the insurance company. *Oh, if only I knew more about the way he works*, she thought. Anyway, she knew that when he returned home that evening, he'd explain, and everything would be all right.

The afternoon crawled. She couldn't concentrate. Her brain raced. Her head ached. Her heart pounded so loudly she felt sure that everyone else in the office would be able to hear it.

It was raining when she left. So much for believing that sunshine forecast. Her umbrella was in the hall cupboard at home. Every passing car threw up spray, spattering her legs. The bus came late. She sat hunched, her skirt drenched and clinging to her knees in damp, uncomfortable folds. Mud squelched as she ran along the grass verge and up the path of the old Victorian terrace that had been converted into tiny flats.

Her wet fingers fumbled with the front door key, rain dripping from her hair and down her forehead. She raced up the stairs to the door of their flat and unlocked it. Inside, it was silent and dark. Steve wasn't back yet.

Emma kicked off her shoes in the hallway and went straight into the bathroom. Dragging off her soaking clothes, she turned on the shower and stood under it, feeling the hot water creep over her chilled body.

As she dried herself, she could see her face blurred by steam on the mirror, mascara panda eyes, mouth trembling, lower lip chewed.

Slipping on a towelling robe, she sleeked back her damp hair and padded into the kitchen to make coffee. Holding the mug in both hands, warming them while she sipped it, she went into the bedroom to find fresh clothes. In the doorway, she stopped.

Every drawer was open. The wardrobe, too. The bed was still unmade from this morning, duvet slipped sideways. Steve always took more than his share. The pillows lay dented, hers resting against his. The alarm clock on the bedside table was gone—and so was Steve's dressing-gown from behind the door.

Emma went back to the bathroom. The steam had cleared now. She opened the cabinet. No razor. Only one toothbrush—hers—stood in the glass tumbler. Even the tube of toothpaste was gone. His aftershave. Everything. Gone.

Her legs crumpled and she sank down onto the bathroom stool as the realisation sliced through her. Steve had gone.

But he couldn't have done. Steve wouldn't do a thing like that. He'd been called away! That was it. Many times during their brief married life, he'd received a phone call to go somewhere. Unexpectedly. One of the companies he worked for had some disaster and needed him, immediately.

There'd be a note. She gripped the edge of the washbasin and dragged herself upright. The kitchen! That's where it would be. She hadn't noticed it in her haste to get warm again.

So why didn't he phone me at work? The thought worried her.

On leaden legs, she walked into the kitchen, her eyes searching. It must have fallen onto the floor. A draught when she opened the door, maybe. She knelt, scanning every inch.

The living room. Of course—that's where it would be. How stupid of her not to look there first.

There was a space where the portable television had stood. Another for the DVD player and box of DVDs. Books leaned sideways on the shelves, trying to fill empty gaps. The wall clock was gone. Emma turned slowly, eyeing the room, mentally listing missing objects.

But there was no note.

It was impossible. Steve wouldn't do this. She knew him too well for that. Or did she?

They'd been married for three months, and met only weeks before that. A whirlwind romance. But you know, don't you, if you've fallen in love? And Emma was quite sure. There'd never been anyone like Steve in her life before. He was the most fantastic man she'd ever met. At thirty, he was almost ten years older, but even so, it had been instant attraction—for both of them. She knew he adored her. He kept telling her so—and men don't say things like that unless they mean it, do they?

Emma went back into the kitchen and made more coffee. Black, with plenty of sugar. Caffeine. That's what you needed for clear thought. And sugar, for shock.

Back in the sitting room, she perched on the arm of the sofa, staring around, sipping the strong dark liquid.

And then she realised. It was so obvious. The open drawers and wardrobe. The missing items. They meant only one thing. Burglary.

The flat had been ransacked! Someone had broken in and stolen everything of value.

But the money withdrawn from the bank?

Ice crept down her spine. Steve must have been there that morning when they came! They'd forced him to go to the bank with them and draw out that money. So where was Steve now?

Her heart lurched. Had they taken him with them? Not as a hostage, though. What use would he be? They already had the money. So there was only one thing they could do. Steve would have seen their faces. Could describe them. Her imagination raced on. That meant . . .

Hot coffee splashed over her legs as she stood up quickly. The police. She had to phone the police. Maybe it wasn't too late. Maybe Steve was still alive. He *had* to be alive.

She was shaking so much she could barely press the keys. Nine, nine . . .

'Which service do you require?' The response was clipped and efficient.

'Police. It's urgent. Please hurry.'

The deep tones of a man answered. Calm. Strangely reassuring.

'My husband's been kidnapped. They're going to kill him.'

'Now, madam, just slow down. What's your name?'

'Emma, Emma Taylor. No, sorry. Emma Jones. Mrs Jones.'

'Your address, please?'

'You must do something! Quickly!'

His voice was quiet and soothing. 'We will, but first I need to know a little more, Mrs Jones. Now, where exactly do you live?'

She stammered out the address, panic tearing through her. Steve could already be dead, while this man was wasting time asking

10

questions.

'Right, Mrs Jones. There's a squad car on its way to you now. If I could just take a few more details.'

She could hear the wail of a siren, see the flash of lights reflected on the ceiling, and dropped the phone. Within seconds she was out of the flat, down the stairs and opening the front door. Two figures stood in the rain—a stern-looking woman in uniform and a younger man, wearing a dark suit.

Her eyes scanned their warrant cards while the man spoke. 'Detective Inspector Goring and Police Constable Cole. Now, Mrs Jones,' he said gently, as they climbed the stairs. 'You say your husband's been kidnapped? That he's about to be killed?'

'I've told someone everything on the phone!' Emma shrieked. 'Why aren't you out there looking for him?'

'I'll make us all a cup of tea, shall I, Emma?' the policewoman said.

The Inspector's smile was reassuring. 'I'm afraid I do need to know exactly what happened. Step by step, Mrs Jones. Without that, we can't even begin a search for your husband. Now, let's start at the beginning.'

Nails pressing into her palms, Emma tried to keep her voice level.

'I found the flat like this when I got home. Ransacked. And Steve gone.' Three mugs of tea appeared on a tray. Mechanically, she took one, gripping it between her hands. At least it kept them steady.

'You carry on, sir, while I check out the flat,' the female officer said. 'What time did you return home?'

'About ten to six.'

'Was the flat door open?'

Emma shook her head. 'No, it wasn't—I remember I had to unlock it.'

He was jotting down notes in a black leather notebook. 'No break-in, then. Does anyone else have a key?'

'Only my husband.'

The policewoman returned from the bedroom and was moving round the living room, pausing where objects had obviously gone.

'Is anything missing from the bathroom?' she asked.

Emma drank some of the tea, aware that it was unbearably sweet. 'My husband's razor, toothbrush and his toothpaste. You think Steve's just walked out on me, don't you?' she blazed.

'It is unusual for burglars to take such personal items,' the policewoman pointed out. 'Is any money missing, Emma? Credit cards? Building society passbooks? A cheque book, maybe?'

Emma hesitated, anticipating their reaction. 'Fifty thousand pounds was withdrawn from his bank account this morning,' she faltered.

The atmosphere became electric.

'Rather a lot to have in an account, isn't it, Emma?'

The constant use of her first name was beginning to annoy her. 'It was a legacy. My grandmother died six months ago. The cheque arrived on Monday. Tomorrow we were going to look at some houses. There'd be a deposit. Furniture. Steve said we'd need ready cash.'

Emma's throat constricted, reading their thoughts. Tears burned her eyes.

'Don't upset yourself, Emma. There's probably a simple explanation. Where does Steve work? Have you tried to get in touch with him?'

Tea slopped onto the table as Emma slammed down the mug. 'Of course I've tried! It was the first thing I did, but his mobile isn't switched on.'

'Give me the number and I'll try it again. In the meantime, can you tell us who it is he works for?'

Closing her eyes, Emma swallowed. 'He's freelance. An insurance assessor. Different companies employ him. It changes from day to day.'

More glances were exchanged.

The inspector stopped taking notes and raised one eyebrow. 'How long have you been married, Mrs Jones?'

'Three months, but what's that got to do with it?' she demanded. 'Look, Inspector, something has happened to my husband and you're making no effort whatsoever to find him.'

'We will, Mrs Jones. But we need to have a clear picture of events first. Can we just go over these details again?'

He turned back a couple of pages in his notebook and started to read. 'Around midday today you discovered fifty thousand pounds had been withdrawn from your husband's bank account. On returning home at approximately seventeen fifty hours, you found items to be missing from the flat that you share, but no apparent forced entry. Personal items belonging to your husband, Steven Jones, including all clothing, are also missing.'

He paused, while she waited, stomach churning.

'And the mobile number given to you by Steven Jones is non-existent.'

'What?' she gasped.

'We've had it checked out and there's no such number, I'm afraid.'

'Then you've written it down wrongly.'

'May I check it again with the one in your diary?'

She fished in her bag, riffled through the pages and read it out carefully.

He shook his head. 'There's no record of such a number.'

'Then *I* must have written it down incorrectly. Misplaced a digit, or something.

It's easy to do.'

His blue eyes were solemn. 'Maybe.'

Emma sat up straight in her chair. 'You believe that Steve's taken the money and everything, and left me, don't you?'

'It's a possibility, Emma,' the policewoman said gently. 'What do you know about his background? Is he a local man? How long have you known him? What about his family? Hobbies? Friends?'

Emma felt as though life was draining out of her. She could answer none of the questions. She'd never even thought to ask Steve. They loved each other. Nothing else mattered.

Until now.

When they stood up, she saw the man was a head and shoulders taller than his female colleague. Leanly built. Cheekbones sharply accentuating the contours of his face. His eyes were filled with compassion when he looked at Emma. It surprised her.

'We'll work on the information you've given us, Mrs Jones,' he said, slipping the notebook into a pocket of his suit. 'But I think you can rest assured that nothing violent has happened to your husband. I doubt he's been abducted. It would appear that, maybe, he's left— temporarily.'

He turned in the doorway. 'Oh, just one more thing. Does your husband have a car?'

Hope flared through her. 'Yes. Yes, he does. A Ford Focus. White.'

15

'Do you know the registration number?'

Trying to remember, Emma closed her eyes. 'Wait a minute! We went on honeymoon in it. There are some photos.'

She scrabbled through the bookshelves, fearing that Steve had taken the album, too. But he hadn't. Pulling it out, she flicked through the pages.

'Look. The car's in the background of this one.' Her heart sank. 'But it's too far away, isn't it? The number is blurred. Impossible to read.'

For a moment, his hand rested beside hers on the table, as he studied the page. It was a strong hand, she noticed, with long tapering fingers, the back of it covered in a faint scattering of dark hairs.

'Can I borrow this photo? There's a chance we can enhance that number plate to a readable standard.'

She eased the picture from its transparent sleeve.

'Would you say this is a good likeness of your husband, Mrs Jones?'

She stared down at the picture of Steve. Casually dressed in jeans and a vivid green sweatshirt. Fair hair ruffled by the wind. His brown eyes laughing back at her. How could he be a liar and a cheat?

'Yes,' she said, looking up into the steady blue gaze that met hers. 'It's a very good likeness of Steve.'

The Inspector's smile was comforting. 'Then there's a very good chance that we'll be able to trace your husband as well.'

CHAPTER TWO

Emma didn't sleep that night. How could she? Her mind seethed. Were the police right about Steve? Was he a thief? A deceiver? *And what does that make me?* she wondered. *Loving him? Trusting him?*

As it was Saturday she didn't need to get up early. What was the point anyway, now? She huddled miserably under the covers.

Just before midday, the phone rang. Flinging the duvet aside, she scrambled to answer it.

'Steve?' she asked breathlessly.

'Good morning, Mrs Jones. It's DI Goring.'

'Who?' Her brain was filled with confusion.

'Tim Goring. We met yesterday. With regard to your missing husband.'

'Oh—the policeman?'

'Yes, Mrs Jones. The policeman.'

For a moment she thought she could hear amusement in his voice, but when he spoke again his tone was serious. 'I've had that photograph blown up. Of the car. Remember? Its registration number is quite clear now.' There was a silence, before he continued.

17

'From that, we've traced the owner.'

A great surge of happiness winged through her. 'So that's it—you've found Steve, then!'

'I think it would be better if I came and spoke to you direct, Mrs Jones. It's never easy talking over the phone. Would that be convenient? If I arrived in ten minutes or so?'

'Could you make it half an hour? I've just got up. I need a shower.'

'Half an hour, then.'

After he'd rung off and she was in the shower, Emma's happiness gave way to doubts. There were so many questions she should have asked him.

Where had they found Steve? Was he all right? What couldn't DI Goring tell her over the phone? It must mean Steve was hurt. Or badly injured. Dead, even! They wouldn't give out news like that over the phone, would they? Someone had to be there, with her, when she was told the worst. Ten minutes, the Inspector had said, so it must be urgent. Wouldn't that mean bad news?

Soap stung her eyes. She buried her face in the towel and began to get dried, turning over their conversation in her mind.

From that we've traced the owner.

The owner. Why didn't he say Steve's name? But he hadn't mentioned Steve by name at all. Hadn't actually said that Steve had been found. Just that they'd traced the owner of the Ford Focus.

It was thirty-five minutes before DI Goring arrived. By that time Emma was frantic with anxiety.

It wasn't a police vehicle this time, but a mud-spattered blue car. An Astra, she decided. Her brother had one like that. From the window she watched it draw up outside and the dark head of the Inspector emerge.

As if sensing she was looking out, he glanced up and she saw him raise a hand in greeting. Then his long legs were striding towards the front steps and she flew down to let him in. For such a thin man, he seemed to fill the hallway as he came through, bending slightly to avoid the door frame.

Suddenly, she didn't want to hear what he was going to say. She knew it was bad news. He looked so serious. Maybe he always looked serious. In his job, there couldn't be much to be joyful about.

'Would you like a cup of tea? Or coffee?' she asked, wanting to delay what he had to tell her.

'Coffee would be good. No sugar.' He followed her into the kitchen.

With shaking hands, she took a jar from the cupboard. 'I'm afraid I've only got instant.'

'That's fine by me.' He smiled, and she could see by the pattern of lines crinkling out from his eyes that it was something he frequently did. Maybe she was wrong about him being serious.

'People always do that, don't they?' he said. 'Apologise for it being instant coffee.' He pulled out one of the stools from the breakfast bar, then hesitated before sitting down. 'May I?'

Emma nodded, pouring boiling water into two mugs and stirring the granules. 'Milk is in the jug.'

His gaze held hers as he took a mug. 'I'm sorry, but it's not good news. I think you've probably already guessed that much, though, haven't you?'

'It's like a terrible nightmare,' she said, her voice faltering.

'But with a nightmare,' he said gently, 'you always wake up and find it's not real. I'm afraid this is very real. And not at all pleasant.'

Emma covered her mouth with her hand, trying to stop it from quivering. 'Then tell me quickly. Please.'

'From a blow-up of the photograph we were able to read the registration number clearly. The owner of that Ford Focus is Steven Matthew Jones.'

A tremendous wave of relief swept through her. 'Steve!' she cried out.

DI Goring picked up his mug, sipped the coffee, and carefully put it down on the table again. 'We've done a check on Steven Matthew Jones.' He paused, while his blue eyes studied her face for a moment.

'And?' she said impatiently.

Ruefully, he pushed out his lip. 'You're not going to like the next bit.'

'Oh, for goodness' sake get on with it.'

'The address given isn't this one.'

'So?' she said, unwrapping a packet of digestive biscuits and holding it out to him. 'He obviously didn't bother to change it when he moved in here.'

The Inspector took a biscuit and put it beside his mug. 'His current address is in Surrey—where he resides with his wife, Alison Margaret Jones, and their two children, Mark David aged three years four months and Charlotte Anne, aged ten months.'

Emma stared blankly back at him, crumbs scattering from the packet in her trembling hand.

'This must be a divorced wife.' Automatically she brushed the crumbs into a tidy heap on the table. 'Steve's married to me.'

'There's been no divorce. And they do live together.'

'But they can't!' Emma blazed, slamming her hand down, sending biscuits everywhere. 'Steve lives here with me. He can't be in two places at once. You've made a mistake. It must be someone with a similar name.'

'Do you have a marriage certificate, Mrs Jones?'

'Of course I have!' The stool crashed to the floor as Emma jumped up and went into the living room. She knew exactly where it was—

tucked into a special pocket in their wedding photo album.

For a second her hand hesitated as she picked up the book. Would Steve . . . But it was there. Neatly folded. Triumphantly, she returned to the kitchen and handed it to the Inspector. He put down his half-eaten biscuit and opened up the paper.

'See!' she said. 'Emma Louise Taylor, aged twenty-one years. Steven Matthew Jones, aged thirty years. And the address of this flat. All perfectly legal. And here's the name of the Register Office, so you can go and check, which I'm sure you will.'

His jawline hardened. 'You do realise what this means, don't you?'

'Yes,' she replied in wild relief. 'It means that you've got the whole thing completely wrong.'

He raised one eyebrow and she saw his mouth twist wryly sideways.

'I don't think so. If all this is correct, then the man's a bigamist as well.'

'Don't be ridiculous!'

'How else do you explain it, then?'

Emma gave him a condescending smile. 'It's really quite simple, Detective Inspector Goring. There are two entirely different men, who just happen to have the same name. So instead of sitting there, drinking coffee, maybe you should go and get it sorted.'

He rose to his feet, his head catching the

hanging light, sending its lampshade into a whirl. 'I'll be in touch.'

'When you have something positive to report, I hope,' Emma replied, as sarcastically as she could.

He held out his hand, but she ignored it.

After he'd left, Emma went into the bedroom and put on her jacket. The library would be open by now, and there they kept a complete set of UK telephone directories.

*   *   *

It was raining again. Driving rain that blew her umbrella sideways, so that it penetrated every gap in her clothing and ran down the back of her neck. The windows of the Library were misted. Vague shapes loomed inside. She pushed open the heavy door and went into its warmth.

Rows of directories were lined up on shelves at one end. She tugged out the Surrey volume and carried it to a table. An elderly gentleman reading a newspaper glared as the book thumped down, fluttering his pages.

Jackson. James. Jenkins. Jones. There were pages of Joneses. Emma flipped through until she found the column listing *Jones S.* Her finger travelled down it.

And there it was, right at the bottom of the list. Jones, Steven M.

Scrabbling through her bag to find her

diary, she opened it at a blank page, then tried to find a pen. Why were there so many sections to the wretched bag? she fumed. None held her pen. She looked at the elderly gentleman. The pocket of his tweed jacket revealed the cap of a ballpoint.

'Excuse me,' she whispered. 'Could I borrow your pen for a moment?'

He frowned, then tugged it out and passed it across the table.

The directory had closed, losing the page. Emma found it again and copied out the address and telephone number. Snapping the book shut, she went to put it back on the shelf.

'Hey! My pen!' The words echoed loudly through the silence of the room. Turning, she handed it to the man, with a murmured apology.

Epsom. This Steven M. Jones lived in Epsom, Surrey. Fifty or so miles away. Just over an hour's drive. No problem dividing his life between two wives; that's what Detective Inspector Goring would be thinking. But this wasn't her Steve. She knew that. This was a man with the same name—and she was going to prove it once and for all to that over-confident policeman.

*   *   *

By late afternoon, Emma was outside Epsom station where taxis were lined up, waiting,

24

slowly moving away as they filled. She had no choice other than to take one. The address could be anywhere in Epsom—and she didn't know the town.

'Visiting friends?' the driver asked, easing the car into the traffic.

'A relative,' she lied.

'Nice area, that is.'

'Is it?' she answered automatically.

She could see him eyeing her in the mirror. 'Not been here before, then?'

'No, I haven't.'

They were passing the white grandstand of the race-course. Huge areas of grass swept away. The whine of a model plane droned. Dogs barked as they raced up the slope of the hill or leapt round their owners. Children flew kites. Two young girls on rough-coated ponies waited to cross the road.

Emma swayed as the taxi swung round a roundabout and headed into open country. They were passing houses half-hidden in tree-filled gardens.

'This is it, love. Five pounds fifty pence. Want me to pick you up later?'

She found her purse and counted out six pound coins. 'No, thanks. I'm not sure how long I'll be.'

'Have a card, then. Telephone number's on that. Take care.'

He stretched a hand out through the taxi window to slam the door behind her, then shot off back down the road.

The gate creaked open as she pushed it. A gravel drive led up to the house. Parked in front of it was a white Ford Focus. It was Steve's car. Even if she didn't recall its registration number, Emma recognised the vehicle.

One door had a deep scrape running from back to front. The lanes in Devon, where they'd spent their honeymoon, were narrow, the hedges sometimes hiding rough stone walls. Trying to avoid an oncoming tractor, Steve had pulled in too close—and finished up with a damaged door. It would have been expensive to have resprayed, and so the mark remained.

No two cars would have exactly the same damage in exactly the same place. This car had to be Steve's. Emma stepped round it and approached the front door. From somewhere inside she heard a melodious chime as she pressed the bell.

Instantly she regretted the action. What was she going to say when she saw him again? All the fiery enthusiasm that had sent her rushing there to prove that policeman was wrong began to ebb away. But now it was too late. The bell continued its melody.

'Alison's not in. I saw her leave in the car about ten minutes ago.'

Emma turned. A woman was leaning on the wall between the houses.

'She'll be collecting Mark from nursery school. He comes out about this time. Shouldn't be long, though. Little Charlotte is due for her feed soon.'

Emma felt as if the blood was draining from her as Inspector Goring's words pulsed through her head *where he resides with his wife, Alison Margaret Jones, and their two children, Mark David aged three years four months and Charlotte Anne aged ten months.*

She realised the neighbour was still speaking. 'You know she's expecting another one, do you? Bit quick, I think. Charlotte's only ten months, but once the early days are over, it'll be nice to have them all close in age, I suppose.' The woman pushed back a strand of greying hair that had blown across her forehead. 'I've only got the one. Quite enough for me. Never know where he is, half the time. Will you hang on until she gets back?'

'No,' Emma murmured faintly. 'I won't wait. It doesn't matter. I was just . . . passing by.'

'Can I give Alison a message then?' the woman persisted. 'Tell her you were here?'

Shaking her head, Emma stepped swiftly towards the gate, carefully closing it behind her. She'd only walked a few metres when a red estate car drove past and stopped outside the house.

Emma watched as a young, well-rounded girl in a long white tee-shirt and black trousers climbed out, then leaned back inside to lift out a chubby baby, tucking it onto her hip while she guided a little boy through the gate and up the path.

CHAPTER THREE

Emma walked. She didn't know where. Every road looked the same. Drizzle hung like mist, slowly soaking into her jacket. She could feel a hole growing in the toe of her tights. Eventually a bus headed towards her, and she waved it down. It wasn't an official stop, but the driver took pity on her. Luckily it was going towards the town.

The shops were closed now, windows brightly lit, shining out over the damp pavements. A waft of frying drifted from a burger restaurant, but she wasn't hungry. She felt she'd never be hungry again.

How could Steve do this to me? she wondered. *I trusted him. Loved him so much. What will happen to my life now? Not that it matters any more. Steve was my life. Without him, it's pointless.*

At the station, she watched the train wavering through the misty haze. Her body leaned forward, but an elderly woman standing beside her caught her elbow, tugging her back.

'Careful, dear. Can't have you falling onto the line, can we? Nasty mess that would make.' She gave a friendly chuckle, folding her umbrella as she climbed aboard the train. Emma followed her miserably into the carriage.

In the darkened glass of the window, she could see the image of Alison Jones, baby cuddled against her side, her little boy trotting beside her.

How could Steve have cheated on both of us like that? Emma asked herself. Living two completely separate lives. It was impossible to imagine.

Thoughts whirled through her head. *Did he find it difficult to juggle his two lives? Surely he must have done. But why did he do it?*

Was he back there? At the house? Did he see me coming up the path? Or, now that he has all that money, has he left Alison and their children too, to start a completely new life somewhere else? With someone else? Yet another woman who has fallen under his spell?

'Feeling all right, dear?'

The voice broke into Emma's thoughts, and she saw the elderly woman opposite lean forward, her eyes filled with concern.

'I'm fine. Bit of a headache, that's all.'

'Thought you looked a bit peaky. Got far to go?'

Emma shook her head and closed her eyes, resting her head

'That's it, dear. Have a little snooze. Do you a power of good. Mind you don't go past your station, though.'

Once home again, Emma found the answering machine was blinking. Steve! It must be. He'd left her a message. Now all would be explained. Eagerly she pressed the key.

It was Inspector Goring, asking her to contact him as soon as she returned home. No way was she going to do that. There was nothing he could tell her that she didn't already know.

Dragging off her clothes, she fell into bed, and slept.

*   *   *

She guessed who it was, even before she picked up the phone the following day.

'Good morning, Mrs Jones. It's Tim Goring.'

'You've got the name wrong, Inspector,' she answered bitterly. 'I'm not "Mrs" anyone. I never was. You were right. Steve does have a wife and two children.' Tears choked her. 'I've seen them. They're a lovely family.'

'I'm coming round.'

'Don't bother. You've proved your point.'

His voice was firm. 'I said, I'm coming round.'

She curled back into bed, dragging the duvet up, covering her face, feeling tears soak into the soft material. He'd have a wasted journey. She wasn't going to let him in.

When the front door bell rang, she pulled the duvet over her head, trying to shut out the sound. It continued to ring. Shrilly. Insistently. Non-stop.

She heard the Inspector's voice calling from the street outside. 'Emma! I know you're there, and I've no intention of going away.'

Her downstairs neighbour shuffled along the hallway. The ringing ceased.

Footsteps thundered up the stairs. A fist hammered on her door. Twisting the duvet round her body, Emma reluctantly went to open it.

'Are you all right?' Inspector Goring's expression was taut as he almost fell into the room.

'Of course I'm all right.'

He steadied himself, one hand against the door frame.

'I just wasn't sure what you'd . . .'

She pulled the duvet more closely round her bare shoulders. 'Do?' she interrupted. 'Well, I haven't jumped off the nearest bridge—yet.'

Shutting the door, he followed her into the kitchen. 'You look dreadful! You haven't done anything stupid, have you? Taken anything?'

'Overdosed, you mean? Of course not.'

'I'll make some coffee. Sit down.'

The gentle authority in his voice sent tears sliding down her cheeks as she sank onto a stool. Then, helplessly, she was doubled

31

up, sobs wrenching her body, and there was nothing she could do to stop them.

She heard him fill the kettle, switch it on, then the rattle of mugs. A spoon clinked against glass.

His hand smoothed the tangled hair away from her face. Through tear-wet eyes, she could see his head level with hers, as he sank down onto his heels, holding out a handful of paper tissues. Still shuddering with sobs, she rubbed at her eyes and blew her nose. 'I'm sorry.'

He smiled. 'Nothing to be sorry about. You've had a tremendous shock. Drink this. I've put in plenty of milk, so it shouldn't be too hot.'

Her teeth chattered against the rim of the mug.

'So, let me get this right—you actually went over to his house yesterday and saw his wife and children?'

Emma nodded, and sipped the warm liquid. 'Not to speak to. I couldn't do that. I knew it was them, from what you'd said.' She rested the mug on her knee. 'You were quite right. But how could Steve do such a thing? He's got a lovely family. How can he do this to us all?'

Tim Goring stood up, his shoulders drooping as he sighed. 'I really don't know, Emma. The more I learn about people, the more they amaze, and frequently horrify, me.' He studied her thoughtfully, then frowned.

32

'When did you last have something to eat?'

She shrugged. 'Oh, I don't know. Yesterday. Maybe the day before. I can't remember.'

He opened the fridge and took out a box of eggs. 'Saucepans under here?' he asked, searching beneath the sink.

'What are you doing?'

'Making scrambled egg. Quick. Simple. Easy to digest. Butter in the fridge, here, is it?'

Emma perched on the stool, watching as he switched on the cooker, broke eggs into a saucepan, added milk and a knob of butter and began to beat them with a fork.

'I don't want anything to eat.'

'Well, I could do with something. Bread go in here?' He pushed two slices into the toaster. 'Whoops,' he said, picking up the saucepan. 'Why does it always stick to the bottom? Do you like salt and pepper?'

Deftly he buttered the toast and slid it onto two plates, then spooned out the creamy egg. It smelled and looked delicious and as Emma cut into a slice, she realised suddenly how hungry she was.

'You'll feel better after that.'

'Don't they feed you at the police station?' she asked, watching as he put more bread into the toaster.

'Not like this—and besides, I'm off duty today.'

'Off duty? So what are you doing here?'

'I was worried about you. You didn't ring

33

back last night, and guessing the state you'd be in after seeing Steve's family . . . '

Emma took one of the hot slices of toast he handed her. 'Do you take all your cases so seriously?'

'No.' He smiled, and bit into the toast, and she noticed the laughter lines crinkling the corners of his eyes. 'But then, not many of my cases are quite as interesting as this one.'

*   *   *

'Someone will have to visit Alison Jones and talk to her.' Tim Goring was scrubbing the remains of the scrambled egg from the bottom of the saucepan while he spoke.

'Does she have to know?' Emma asked, drying a plate with a tea-towel. 'It will tear her apart.'

His mouth twisted wryly. 'She'll have to know eventually. There's no way to avoid it, I'm afraid, Emma. He's a bigamist—and a conman.'

'She'll be devastated. Hearing what he's done. I know how I feel and I haven't even given birth to a family with him.' Emma picked up another plate and began to dry it. 'Don't you hate your job at times like this?'

'I don't create the crimes. My job is to catch and stop those who do.' He swilled clean water round the sink. 'And when I see the trauma that man has put you through, it makes me all

34

the more determined to track him down.'

Towering over her, he rested his hands on the edge of the sink. 'That man's a criminal, Emma. He tricked you into marriage, with the purpose of stealing your money. Who knows how many other unsuspecting women he's done the same to? And will continue doing, I have no doubt—until he's caught and put behind bars.'

'Behind bars?' Horrified, Emma stared up into his steely blue eyes. 'You mean—prison?'

'Bigamy is a serious crime, and so is theft.'

'But Steve's not a criminal!'

'Of course he is! And he has to be brought to justice.'

Her chin jutted. 'Then there's no way I'm going to help you. Doesn't it trouble your conscience, imprisoning someone? How does your wife feel about living with a man who can do that?'

'I no longer have a wife.'

'Well, that's not surprising, is it?'

Seeing the raw pain that flooded into his face, Emma regretted the words as soon as she'd said them.

'My wife was in the police force, too.' His voice faltered, before continuing more slowly. 'She was caught up in a hostage situation. A man holding his girlfriend and their child at gunpoint. My wife put herself between them and him—and he shot her. Deliberately shot her.'

35

Emma watched his throat move as he swallowed.

'It was three days before she actually died and, finally, it had to be my decision that the life-support be switched off. I'll forever wonder whether I made the right decision.'

He turned quickly away as Emma reached out to touch his arm. 'I'm so very sorry. I had no idea.'

He shook her hand off. 'That man ended up having psychiatric treatment, and was eventually freed. He's back living with his girlfriend and they now have a second child. Just as if nothing had ever happened.'

He swung back towards her again, and she saw the taut line of his jaw. 'Which is why, Emma, I have no qualms whatsoever about putting criminals behind bars.'

'But Steve isn't a criminal. He's never hurt anyone.'

'Do you know that?'

She hesitated. 'I know he wouldn't. He's not that kind of man.'

'I dare say the woman hostage once thought that about her boyfriend.'

'There's no comparison!' Emma protested hotly. 'You can't compare Steve with a man who could shoot someone in cold blood.'

'You would forgive him, Emma? After all he's done?'

She lowered her eyes, unable to meet the challenge of his.

'Yes,' she said. 'I would forgive him. I love him—and I'm married to him.'

Inspector Goring shook his head. 'No, Emma. I'm afraid you're not.'

*   *   *

The next few days dragged by while Emma expected the phone to ring, or a letter to arrive. Steve wouldn't just abandon her. He couldn't. Not when he loved her so much. And he did love her—didn't he?

She was still convinced he'd been kidnapped, or forced into something he didn't want to do. But if so, then why had he driven back to Epsom and left his car there?

Inspector Goring hadn't returned. Emma wondered whether, by now, he'd told Alison that her husband was a bigamist—and a thief.

Something else puzzled Emma—why Steve had actually married her. But then she remembered her grandmother's legacy. She'd known when she met Steve that it was forthcoming, once probate was granted, and was so delighted about inheriting such a fortune, she'd told everyone.

Was it the money that had attracted him—not her? And the only way he saw to get his hands on it was to marry her?

There were so many unanswered questions. The whole situation was dragging her down—and then she caught a stomach bug and started being sick. After a week, it wasn't any better, so she went to her doctor for something to settle it quickly.

After giving her a thorough check-over, he smiled. 'Well, Mrs Jones,' he said, rinsing his hands as she got dressed. 'Nothing to worry about there. All quite normal. I should say you're about seven or eight weeks pregnant.'

'Pregnant!' Her jaw dropped and she stared in panic.

'Come a bit sooner than you and your husband had planned, has it? These things do happen, no matter how careful you are. I'm sure you'll both be delighted, as soon as you've got over the initial surprise.'

He added a few notes to her file on the computer, then stood up and walked her to the door. 'Have a word with my receptionist as you go out, will you? She'll fix a date for your scan. Don't look so worried. Everything's just perfect. I'm sure you'll have a beautiful baby.'

*   *   *

A car was drawing away as Emma reached the flat. A dark blue Astra. It reversed, and then Tim Goring's long legs emerged.

'Hi! I just called to see you.' He stopped walking and looked down at her with anxious blue eyes. 'Are you okay?'

'You always seem to be asking me that,' she said. Her voice seemed to come from a long

38

way away, echoing through a spinning mist that was swirling round, growing thicker and thicker. 'And no, I'm not okay. I've just been told I'm pregnant.'

As her legs crumpled, his arm went round her waist, catching her before she fell, and she let herself sink into the welcoming darkness.

'Emma!'

She was sitting at the bottom of the stairs, Tim Goring still holding her, while the downstairs neighbour waved a smelling-bottle under her nose. The pungent shock of ammonia biting into her nostrils startled her and her eyes widened, stinging from the vapour.

'Take it away!' she gasped, pushing out her hand.

'I think she'll be all right now. Thanks, though. You've been a great help. I'll take her upstairs.' Tim's voice was firm, and Emma heard the neighbour mutter something, then her door close.

'I can walk,' she protested, but she was already being swept up in his arms, her head resting against his shoulder, and found she was quite content to remain there as he climbed the stairs.

'Key?' he asked.

Puzzled by a steady thudding in her ear, she murmured, 'Pocket,' and felt her body move sideways as he unlocked the door, before realising the sound was the throb of his heartbeat.

'You're quite a weight for one so slender,' he gasped, putting her down on the sofa.

'I thought policemen had to be fit.'

'Well, this one quite obviously isn't, but then carrying distressed maidens up flights of stairs isn't part of our training. We leave that to firemen. How are you feeling now?'

'That I don't want to be pregnant.'

'It does happen, you know.' He was already in the kitchen, making tea.

'I do know, I just thought it was a tummy bug.'

'A tummy bug!' She heard his laughter and could visualise his eyes crinkling. 'Well, maybe you'll give birth to a beautiful butterfly.'

'Don't joke. I don't find it funny.'

He put his head round the door. 'Sorry, only trying to cheer you up.'

'Nothing will ever cheer me up again. Anyway, what were you coming to tell me about?'

'Hang on a second, the kettle's just boiled.'

Emma swung her legs down from the sofa, rose cautiously to her feet, and went to join him. 'Well?' she said.

'Alison Jones and the children have disappeared.'

'Oh, no! When?'

He carefully placed a mug into her hand. 'Yesterday. Look, sit down on the stool, before you keel over again. Is that tea all right?'

40

'Yes, it's fine.'

Taking a gulp from his own mug, he continued. 'Unfortunately, we've not been keeping a close eye on them. It's Steve we've been looking out for, Anyway, one of our officers went there yesterday to see if Alison had heard anything from him. The white Ford Focus was still in the drive, but not the red estate car you mentioned.'

'Perhaps she was just out somewhere, or taking the little boy to nursery.'

'No. A neighbour said Alison told her they were going away for a while. The whole family, including Steve, left very early yesterday in the estate car.'

'So they're with Steve?' He nodded, picking up the kettle to refill their mugs. 'Then I'm glad.'

Hot water slopped onto the table as he roared, 'You're *what*?'

'They're a lovely family. It would be awful if they weren't all together.'

Tearing off a sheet of kitchen paper, he mopped up the spill. 'I just don't understand you, Emma. After all he's done to you? What about you and your baby? Who's going to look after you?'

'I'll cope.'

He dropped the wet towel into the bin. 'You're not coping very well so far. Passing out like that.'

Emma glared. 'That was shock. I'd just been

told I was pregnant.'

There was a jangle of sound as his mobile rang. Stepping out into the hallway, he answered it, before returning to the kitchen.

'Are you sure you're going to be okay now? I have to get back.'

For a moment his hand rested on hers, then squeezed it lightly. She stared down, feeling its reassuring strength. Tears blurred her vision.

'Yes,' she said, not wanting to look up and meet his eyes. 'I'll be fine.'

When the door had closed behind him, she curled into a heap on the sofa, unable to hold back her tears any longer. She'd wanted a baby so much. Their baby. Hers and Steve's. To be a complete family. And her wish had been granted.

But now—without him—it was the worst thing that could have happened.

CHAPTER FOUR

People say that once you've hit rock bottom, you start to come up again, or give up completely. Emma knew she had to make that choice.

Sunshine woke her, blazing in through the window to dazzle her eyes. Amazingly, she'd slept well that night, still curled up on the sofa. For once, she didn't feel sick. Remembering

Tim Goring's scrambled eggs, she found a saucepan, made some, and enjoyed her breakfast.

Now she had to decide what she was going to do about the baby. It would be so easy to have a termination, but growing inside her was a new life. Growing for seven or eight weeks, that was what the doctor had said. In seven months' time it would be a living being. How could she destroy that?

She tried to picture what it might be. Who it might look like. Steve was quite handsome— or, at least, she thought so—with his thick fair hair and dark brown eyes. Would this baby resemble him? Or her? She pulled a face at herself in the bathroom mirror as she showered.

Her stomach curved slightly, no longer flat. So soon? Why hadn't she realised? But she'd thought her lack of period was due to all the trauma and shock of Steve's disappearance.

She was going to need money now. She couldn't stay in the flat. A baby needs a garden. Somewhere, later, to play. One of those new houses could still be a possibility—if she could afford the deposit.

This was Steve's baby, too. It wasn't just her inheritance that he'd stolen. It belonged to his child as well. If anyone was going to track down Steve, then it would be her. He couldn't just vanish into thin air.

Inspector Goring would have to look to his

laurels, if he was to succeed before she did. His only aim was to put Steve behind bars, but she needed to find him first, and claim back her fifty thousand pounds.

Now, she had a purpose. Two, in fact. Her baby, and finding Steve. Officially, she was still off sick from work with a tummy upset. Time enough to let them know the real reason.

Once again she caught the train to Epsom. Finding the right bus was no problem and it saved a taxi fare. Just as Tim Goring had said, the white Ford Focus was parked in the same place in the drive as she'd last seen it.

Emma rang the bell, just in case they'd returned, and listened to the melodious tune play somewhere inside. No one came. As she turned away, an old Mini shot up the adjoining driveway and stopped, scattering gravel. A tall, loose-limbed boy swung himself out.

'Excuse me,' Emma called, over the low wall. 'Do you know if Alison and Steve are away?'

He started to untie a bicycle from the rear of the car. 'Left a day or two ago,' he said, without turning round.

'Any idea where?'

The boy carefully lowered the bike to the ground. 'She's got a mother or aunt or something down in Cornwall.'

Emma stood still. 'Alison, you mean?'

He nodded. 'Think that's where Mum said they'd gone. Lizard Peninsula. Alison goes

44

down there for a while when Steve is off on one of his mystery tours. Mum keeps an eye on the house.'

'Mystery tours?'

The boy laughed. 'He's never around half the time. Mum reckons he leads a double life.'

If only your mum knew, Emma thought. 'Well, thanks, anyway.'

Cornwall. Emma had stayed there a few times when she and her brother were children. Always in St Ives. Steep, narrow streets with clustered-together shops and cottages. Golden sand. A harbour where boats vied for trade, taking tourists for fishing trips or along the coast to see local beauty spots. Lots of tiny art galleries, where their parents liked to browse. Her father's hobby was painting watercolours.

And once they'd been to Helston on Flora Day. She'd never forget that. The sound of the band. Ladies in elegant long dresses and beautiful hats dancing with top-hatted men, in and out of the houses and shops, up and down the town. That was near the Lizard Peninsula.

It was a long way to go, though, on the off-chance they were there.

At first Emma thought of telling Tim Goring, letting him do all the donkey work. But then she changed her mind. All he wanted was to have Steve sent to prison. If he did, then Alison and the children would have to fend for themselves.

All Emma wanted was to find Steve—and

get back her money. Whatever Steve had done, Emma felt sure Alison had not been part of it. There was no reason for her to suffer. She wondered what tale Steve had told her. How he'd explained why they were going away at short notice.

But they may not even be in Britain, let alone Cornwall, Emma reasoned. With the Channel Tunnel, it wasn't difficult to cross to the continent. Start a new life together there.

By the time she returned to her flat, she was exhausted and hungry. She hadn't eaten since breakfast and now she was eating for two.

Her neighbour met her in the hallway. 'That young man was here again.'

For a moment, Emma thought she meant Steve and her heart lurched.

'The policeman. He left you a message. I haven't read it,' she added quickly. Emma took the folded sheet of paper, smiling her thanks.

'Quite friendly,' the neighbour observed. 'For a policeman, that is.'

Emma climbed the stairs and let herself into the flat, then unfolded the note. The writing was clear and firm, sloping forwards across the page.

Sorry to miss you, Emma. Hope you're feeling better today. Take care. TIM GORING.

Carefully, she refolded it, and slipped it into the pocket of her jeans. *Now for some food*, she thought, and tucked two thick slices of bread into the toaster, while she heated a can of soup. Still hungry afterwards, she made more toast and buttered it. After that, she felt better.

By phoning round she discovered there was a coach, leaving the following day, going direct to Falmouth. From there it wouldn't be difficult to reach the Lizard.

As she drifted into sleep that night, it crossed her mind that Tim Goring might have quicker ways of finding Steve, but the thought of him forlorn in the narrow confines of a prison cell soon convinced her that her plan was a far kinder way.

*   *   *

Falmouth in the sunshine was beautiful. The sea glinted. Boats of all sizes lay on its surface, slowly revolving, until their taut anchor chains compelled them to reverse.

Emma needed somewhere to stay. Somewhere very cheap. The coach driver was helpful, directing her to the far end of the town where a steep hill led to rows of guest houses and small hotels. A single room, though, was not easy to find. With her rucksack growing heavier by the minute, she trudged on up the hill.

And then, as she was beginning to regret ever coming, the woman who answered the dust-covered front door of what had once been two separate semi-detached houses, said she

47

had just one single available.

The price was so cheap, Emma could hardly believe it—until she saw the room. With both arms outstretched, she could touch either wall. The bed was narrow. A wardrobe stood at one end, its door ajar. Under the window was a straight-backed wooden chair. A chest of drawers that didn't match anything was parallel with the bed. Next to it hung a small washbasin, one tap dripping. But what more did she need?

'Oh,' the woman said, as she turned to leave. 'Bathroom is across the corridor. I'll bring a towel next time I come up. Here's your key. Breakfast is seven-thirty. TV lounge is opposite the dining room. Everyone's watching the cricket. Plenty of restaurants in the town if you want an evening meal.'

Emma heard the woman's slippered feet whisper away down the corridor as she lowered her rucksack to the floor, then looked out of the window. Below was a small concrete yard with an ancient shed, its roof felt flapping. A rusting cooker leaned on three legs against a washer without a door. Three old mattresses were propped against the wooden fence, next to a climbing rose that twisted thornily, over the top. One faded yellow flower fluttered.

There were seagulls on the grey slate roofs opposite, standing in rows along the ridge tiles. Every so often one would lean forward, yellow beak opening to squawk loudly. This seemed to annoy the rest and they all joined in ferociously.

But in the distance Emma could see the sea. Just a faint gleam through the swaying branches of a tall pine.

She was hungry. Ravenous, in fact. Her appetite had returned with a vengeance, now she no longer felt sick. Plenty of restaurants in the town, the landlady had said. Dumping her rucksack on the bed, she combed her hair, washed her hands under a thin stream of tepid water, dried them on a paper handkerchief, and went out.

The brightness of the day had gone. Sea mist hung in the air, beading her hair and eyelashes Walking down the hill to the town was far easier than the steep climb up, and it only took her ten minutes to reach the narrow main street, straggled by little shops. Here and there cobbled passageways revealed glimpses of the sea, and its salt smell drifted in with the mist.

At the first restaurant, she stopped and went inside. Warmth, tinged with a mixture of fish, onions, frying and spices closed round her. Relieved not to feel nauseous, she sat down at a table and picked up the menu.

It was almost dark by the time she'd finished her meal. Pinpoints of light winked along the line of the coast. Somewhere a lighthouse sent long beams jetting across the hazy line of the horizon. The restaurant had filled up. Voices murmured, rising at times, mingled with sudden bursts of laughter.

Only Emma sat alone.

Paying for her tasty seafood pie, rich with prawns and a mixture of white fish, followed by a huge bowl of fresh fruit salad hidden under thick Cornish clotted cream, she stepped outside and shivered in the clammy dampness.

On the climb up the hill, she stared in through bay windows where people sat at individual tables, chewing or speaking silent words. *Is every house in this road a small hotel?* she wondered.

At the back of her mind was the hope that, in one of those brightly lit dining-rooms, she'd see Steve and Alison, Mark perched between them, spoon-feeding baby Charlotte in a high chair while they ate their supper.

Real life doesn't allow for such coincidences. Breathlessly, she reached her guest house, tugged the key from her pocket and let herself in.

From the TV lounge, she could hear the raised voice of a newsreader and pushed open the door. Faces turned at the interruption. Not one was welcoming. Every armchair was filled. A map filled the TV screen, dotted with clouds and rays of sunshine. Silently she closed the door.

Back in her room, she sat on the bed. She'd already discovered that the wooden chair had one leg shorter than the other three and wobbled dangerously. A painted tin tray with a mug, plastic kettle and saucer containing three teabags, a tiny pot of milk, a small packet of coffee and another of sugar had appeared on top of the chest of drawers in her absence. But not the promised towel.

Why on earth did I come here? she asked herself. *I've no idea where to start looking and even if I did, Steve and his family are probably not even in Cornwall.* Tim Goring's tall, lean figure loomed into her mind. *Why, oh why, didn't I leave it all to him? It was pointless for me even to try to find Steve. And if I did find him—what then? What would I do? I couldn't just march up and demand he handed back the money he'd stolen.*

But had he in fact legally stolen it? It was in his bank account. He was entitled to withdraw money. Thoughts whirled round and round in her brain, exhausting her. Desperately, she tried to shut them out.

There were lights in the houses opposite. Curtains drawn, like closed eyelids. Where did those seagulls go when it was night-time? Back to the beach? Or did they roost on buildings in the town?

Her head ached. Slowly she undressed, washed in the little basin, then crawled under the duvet. Its thin, faded yellow cover, once patterned with enormous daisy-like flowers, smelt musty.

Through the open window she could hear

voices in the kitchen below and a clatter of crockery. Somewhere close by, a dog barked. The tap dripped. She got out of bed and put her flannel in the washbasin to dull the sound. Finally her eyes closed from sheer weariness, and she slept.

*   *   *

Seagulls woke her. Shrill. Raucous. Their shrieks seemed to fill every inch of the room. Half-light. Not yet dawn.

She pulled the bed-cover up to her chin and tried to go back to sleep, but it was impossible, and once she was awake all her worries flooded back. Why is that final hour before day breaks always such an anxious one? The slightest problem is magnified and grows into a monstrous cloud of horror.

It was no good. She had to get up. Too early to shower, with the rest of the guesthouse still asleep. She dragged on her clothes and went downstairs, unlocked the front door and let herself out.

It was daylight by the time she reached the town and wandered the empty streets. A dustcart rumbled past, stopping to empty bins from outside shops. Two boys on bikes sped off towards the hill, leaning sideways to balance the weight of their newspaper bags. Hunched, asleep, in a derelict shop doorway was a bearded tramp, a scrawny black and

52

white dog stretched across his lap.

Emma didn't know what attracted her to the church. Maybe the faint sound of organ music, or because the door was open, a bicycle propped against it. But as she crossed the road, she saw a large poster on the porch wall—*ARK EXHIBITION*. Surely that should be *Art* Exhibition, she thought, until she read on—*Bring Your Children In To See The Animals.* She unlatched the heavy wooden door, and went inside.

Right at the rear of the church was a huge model ark, with papier mâché animal heads looking through the windows, and a ramp leading up to a door. Emma walked through and out into a wide fenced garden where two Shetland ponies accompanied by several goats, lambs, rabbits, ducks, geese and chickens roamed, happily nibbling or chewing.

'What do you think?' an eager voice asked. Swinging round, she saw a silvery haired vicar coming to join her. 'Our Sunday School children's idea.'

'It's brilliant,' Emma replied, smiling in spite of herself.

'It's only for a week, but we've had so many visitors, we may well repeat it later in the season. Do stay as long as you like, if you don't mind the sound of the organ. Early morning's a good time for the organist to practise. Oh, and do write your comments in the visitor's book as you go out, my dear.'

After stroking one of the ponies and rubbing the ears of the lambs, Emma went back into the church. Near the main door a book lay open on a wooden table, filled with the names of people and their comments. Below it, a ballpoint pen had fallen onto the floor. Emma picked it up and put it back on the page, glancing at it as she did so.

One name stood out, halfway down. She stared at it, refusing to believe what she saw. That great swirling flourish of an S. The heavily accentuated V dipping downwards. *Steve Jones.* No one else would turn the tail of a J into a double curl.

More faintly, in neat script below it, she read *Alison Jones, Mark and Charlotte. The children really enjoyed seeing all the animals and the ark. What a lovely idea.*

Emma couldn't believe it. Steve and Alison had visited the church only the day before. They had written no address, but could they be staying in the town? Or somewhere close by? That really would be stretching coincidence too far. But the boy who lived next door to them had said something about a mother or aunt that Alison stayed with on the Lizard.

Swiftly she scanned the names above and below theirs. Mlle Dupont, with an address in Paris. Sadie and Joel Roots from New York, USA. No name with a local address. She was expecting too much—but at least she knew Steve had been in the town. Might even still be there. It narrowed the field. All she had to do was find him.

If only Tim Goring was here, she thought. *He'd know exactly what to do.* She looked at her watch. Almost eight o'clock. In a fast car . . . Somewhere in the back of her diary, she had his telephone number at the police station.

She should have realised he might not be on duty at that hour of the day. The voice that answered was a woman's. What she said surprised Emma.

'Emma Taylor, you say? Connected with the Steven Jones case? Hang on a second, DI Goring left instructions to be contacted on his mobile should you phone at any time. What's your number? I'll get him to ring you back.'

'I'm in Falmouth.'

'Not to worry, give me the number anyway. If I can't contact him, I'll let you know.'

The town was beginning to come to life. Delivery vans and lorries rumbled along the narrow cobbled street to unload into shops. Voices carried on the still salt air as workmen greeted each other.

A smell of new bread and hot pasties spread from the open door of a baker's, making her tummy groan. Breakfast was being served back at the guesthouse by now. She longed for a cup of strong, fragrant coffee.

When her mobile rang, it made her jump.

'Emma?' Tim Goring's voice was deep with concern. 'Are you all right? What on earth are

55

you doing down in Falmouth?'

'Steve's here.'

His voice changed. 'You're not with him, are you?'

She shook her head, then remembered he couldn't see the gesture. 'No, but I've just seen his name. In the visitor's book of a church. Here. In the town. He was there yesterday. With Alison and the children.'

'You're sure?'

'It's his signature.'

'What's your address?' She told him. 'Telephone number?'

She pulled the crumpled card from her pocket and read it out. 'That's a payphone. My room is too small and horrible to have its own phone.'

'Okay.' Emma could imagine him snapping closed his black leather-bound notebook. 'Promise you won't do anything until I contact you?'

'I can't just sit around, doing nothing all day.'

His soft laughter filled her ear. 'That's what worries me, Emma. Remember, this is a police matter.'

'I married Steve,' she reminded him.

'But he was never your husband, Emma. He's a thief and conman—and a very clever and plausible one, too. Just leave it all to us. Find a deckchair and sunbathe on the beach. Take it easy for a while.'

'Huh!' As if that were possible!

'Emma, please don't do anything stupid.'

'Goodbye, Detective Inspector Goring,' she said firmly, and clicked off her mobile. It continued ringing as she walked back along the street and began to climb the hill.

CHAPTER FIVE

If Steve and his family were in Falmouth, they could be staying in any of the hotels or guesthouses that filled the roads surrounding the town. Unless, of course, they were with the relative their neighbour's son had referred to. Emma despaired of ever finding them. It was like looking for the proverbial needle in a haystack.

But then, she reasoned, she'd had one stroke of luck already. Maybe fate was on her side. Temporarily, at least. Steve was either careless, writing his name like that in the church visitor's book, or full of bravado.

Had he fooled his wife, Alison, into thinking they were on holiday? If so, they would be acting as though they were. Trips to the beach with the children. Visits to local attractions. She might see him anywhere.

Or nowhere. Cornwall is a large area. There are hundreds of beaches and tiny coves. Numerous attractions. Her spirits rose and fell constantly as she made her way back to the guesthouse, feeling very tired after the previous day's long tourney.

Exhaustion suddenly hit her after she'd eaten some breakfast. Back in her room, she lay down on the narrow bed and was asleep within seconds. Even the shrieks of the gulls outside didn't disturb her.

She was on a moor, thick mist swirling round her, blotting out everything. Somewhere, she knew, was Steve. She had to find him. Vaguely she could see his outline. Hear his laughter. Almost touch his hand. Almost, but not quite. Each time she stretched out her fingers, he was gone again

Huge dark clouds were gathering now. She could see them, above the mist around her. Black. Ominous. Soon there would be a storm. She had to find Steve. She was terrified of thunder and lightning.

Years ago, she remembered, she'd seen lightning forking down as she walked home from school. Watched it strike the chimney of one of the neighbouring cottages, and the thatch flare into an inferno.

The face of the old lady, mouth wide as she screamed, frail fists hammering on the window, remained in her memory. She could hear her screaming now. Or was it Steve's laughter? And a terrifying rumble of thunder had started, merging with the sound.

Her eyelids fluttered, and slowly lifted.

Someone was knocking on her bedroom door. From the roofs opposite, gulls squabbled noisily. Pushing a tangle of hair away from her face, she slid off the bed and opened the door.

Tim Goring stood there. For a moment she thought she was still asleep.

'How did you . . .?'

A smile tilted the corners of his wide mouth. 'Doesn't take too long if you drive without stopping,' he said, anticipating her question. 'And it is nearly five o'clock.'

'Five o'clock!' she gasped. 'It can't be! I must've been asleep for hours.'

'And you needed it, I'm sure,' he said, glancing over her shoulder into the room with a look of distaste.

She frowned. 'Should you be here? I mean, in Cornwall? Isn't it up to the local police?'

His smile broadened. 'Well, officially I'm now on holiday, so as you see, I've decided to visit Cornwall. Of course, while I'm here and travelling round, if by chance I happen to come across someone I know the police back home are looking for, well it would be my rightful duty as a police officer . . . '

'It all sounds very devious to me, Inspector Goring,' Emma said, interrupting him.

'Then you have a very suspicious mind, Miss Taylor,' he teased. 'More importantly, have you eaten yet? The woman downstairs told me you've been in all day.'

'I did have some breakfast after I phoned

you, but since then I've been asleep, so no I haven't—and I'm starving again.'

'So am I. Let's go and find a restaurant. I'll wait downstairs until you're ready. There doesn't look room enough for more than one in there.'

Emma grinned. 'It is a dump, isn't it? But I needed somewhere cheap—and this couldn't be cheaper.'

'Five minutes?' he asked, lifting one eyebrow.

'Make it six,' she laughed, closing the door.

Sunshine quivered across the room, reflecting on the mirror. Maybe it was the long sleep, but suddenly Emma felt happy for the first time in days.

*   *   *

'You can't stay in that awful room, Emma.' Tim Goring's voice was firm as his gaze met hers across the cheery red and white checked tablecloth of the restaurant where she'd eaten the previous night.

'Wait until you try to find a single room down here at this time of year,' she retorted, glaring back at him. 'It's impossible.'

He dug his fork into a spiral of pasta. 'I already have somewhere to stay.'

'Oh,' she replied tartly. 'A cell at the local nick?'

A sliver of mushroom slipped from the fork

as he laughed. 'Good one. Nope! A friend of mine owns a holiday house over on the Lizard, at Coverack, so I'll be able to use that.'

Emma sipped her orange juice. 'Lucky you.'

'You can join me if you like.'

Her back stiffened.

'Don't look at me like that,' he said, putting down his fork. 'There are three floors and six bedrooms. At least you'll be far more comfortable than where you're staying now. And I can keep an eye on you.'

'Keep an eye on me!' she blazed. 'I guessed there'd be a catch in it. And I thought you were being kind.'

'I am,' he said mildly. 'Be honest, Emma. What were you planning to do? Check out every hotel and guesthouse in the West Country for Steve?'

She glowered at him across the table. *Why does he always have to be so right?* she thought crossly.

'It would take you a month of Sundays, or longer, wouldn't it? Well, it's already happening. His photograph is being circulated by email or fax to every one of them.' He wrinkled his nose. 'What we can't do, though, is check out friends or relations Steve and his family might be staying with.'

Emma sighed. 'Which is most likely where they'll be, if their neighbour's son was right. It's an impossible task, Tim. Even you, with all your resources, won't be able to find him.'

'Nothing is impossible, Emma,' he replied quietly. 'All it takes is time.'

'Which is precisely what we don't have. Steve's not likely to hang around waiting for you to catch up with him.'

'Well, he's not exactly being very careful, is he? Writing his name in a church visitor's book is asking to be caught. But maybe he's the sort of guy who gets a kick from taking risks.'

'Like having two wives?' Emma said wryly.

'Sure you won't have a glass of wine?' Tim held up the carafe and Emma guessed he was adroitly trying to change the subject.

'You're forgetting I'm pregnant,' she replied. 'Alcohol is banned.'

'I'm sorry.' His slanting blue gaze levelled with hers across the table. 'Well, are you going to accept my offer of accommodation?'

She watched the wine swirl into his glass, candlelight reflected in its rosy depths. Saw his lips close over the rim and the long column of his neck move slightly as he swallowed. Reluctantly, she drew her gaze away.

It was a very tempting offer. Anything would be, she decided, compared with that dreadful room at the guesthouse. But did she want to be in such close contact with Detective Inspector Goring? Her gaze lingered on him for a moment more, while she tried unsuccessfully to fight off every sense in her body that was telling her she did.

Abruptly, he pushed back his chair and

62

stood up, and the waiter hurried across the room to hand him the bill.

'Tell me my share,' Emma said quickly, picking up her bag.

'You can pay the tip,' he replied, and she was aware of a sparkle of humour in his eyes.

'But—' She began to protest.

He lifted her jacket from a hook. 'Never argue with a policeman, Emma. Now, are you walking back to that guesthouse, or do I drive you there to collect your things?'

Slipping her arms into the sleeves of her jacket as he held it, she was aware of his hands resting momentarily on her shoulders. Only a slight gesture, but one that sent a wave of heat scalding over her skin.

'Did you say that Coverack was on the Lizard? Is it very far from here?'

'About half an hour's drive.'

'Then I'll come with you,' she said, adding quickly, 'You never know, Steve might be there.'

The woman in charge at the guesthouse looked knowingly from one to the other of them, a faint smile on her face, as Emma paid what she owed.

'Should charge you to the end of the week, you know. Single rooms are much in demand.'

'Not one like that,' Tim ground out, picking up Emma's rucksack.

The woman shot him a ferocious glare. 'Maybe I should charge you for the use of the bed as well, sir.'

Ignoring her, Tim caught hold of Emma's elbow and propelled her towards the door. Once inside his car, she saw his mouth quivering.

'It was insulting, not funny,' she stormed.

His laughter bubbled over. '"Maybe I should charge you for the use of the bed as well, sir",' he mimicked. 'What a woman! There wasn't room for one person to turn over, let alone any hanky-panky.'

Emma hunched herself into her jacket. 'You're as bad as she is.'

She watched his white teeth close over his upper lip, trying to control his laughter. 'I'm sorry, Emma. But really, can you imagine it?'

The problem was that Emma could, and the idea was extremely appealing. It remained with her as the car wound its way along the lanes, past green fields stretching away into the distance. Occasionally she saw the ruins of old engine houses, their tall round chimneys rising up like fingers to indicate where once there had been active tin and copper mines.

Even now miles of tunnels must lie deep below those fields, she thought, *slowly falling into neglect, filling with water. Haunted, maybe, by the ghosts of long-dead miners.*

A helicopter clattered low overhead as if leading the way when they passed Helston, and she saw the long wire fence enclosing the Air Sea Rescue base. The road swung to the left,

64

becoming narrower, hedges hiding stone walls, crowded on either side.

'What are those?' she asked, seeing enormous round discs set on metal structures rise high above them on one side.

'That's the Earth Satellite Station. Used to be quite important at one time for communications all over the world,' he replied. 'Strange place, is Cornwall. Ancient standing stones and the ruins of old mines in one field, and modern things like that and all the wind farms in others.'

The road meandered on through moorland, pink with heather, until it reached a fork, and Tim swung the car to the right, where soon it began to descend a very steep and winding hill. Emma's lips parted in delight as she saw a smooth expanse of sea shimmering in the evening sunshine.

Whitewashed cottages and houses clustered at its edge, separated by a wide granite wall that curved high above a rock-strewn sandy beach. In the distance she could see fishing-boats nudging each other in the horseshoe shelter of a tiny harbour.

'Coverack,' Tim breathed, easing the car through a street narrowed by ambling people. 'Isn't it beautiful?'

It was, but Emma's eyes were already scanning every face they passed. Could one of them be Steve?

The car stopped close to the sea wall,

opposite a small shop with paintings, knick-knacks and tee shirts filling its windows. Tim swung his long body out and stood up. 'I'll just collect the key.'

Emma watched him stride into the shop and saw him smile as he spoke to a bespectacled lady behind the counter just inside, seeing her expression change to welcome him.

There were rocks below the wall, where it curved on up the steep hill. Slow waves rose over them with a thud and wisps of spray that sparkled in the sunshine. Watching them had a hypnotic effect and Emma felt her eyelids begin to droop.

'Okay then? Ready to go?'

She jerked awake. Tim was back in the car and restarting the engine.

'The house is just up there. See. Above the sea.'

It was a long, whitewashed house, three storeys high, facing the bay. Its windows were thick with salt, turning the light coming through them to a haze. Tim carried Emma's rucksack and his own roll-bag into the narrow hall, bending his head in his now-familiar way to avoid the low ceiling. A faint scent of pot pourri filled each room as they opened the doors, discovering where everything was kept.

'Are you sure you're all right, Emma?' His expression was anxious. 'You look exhausted. Go and choose yourself a bedroom while I put the kettle on. I'll bring you up a cup of tea, if you want to rest.'

'Rest! For goodness' sake, Tim! Live in the present.' She snatched her rucksack from him and heaved it over her shoulder. 'I'm not some fragile Victorian lady about to have the vapours or something.'

'Fine! Calm down. But you do look washed out. All this must be quite a strain on you, without . . .'

'Just go and put the kettle on, please, Tim.'

The staircase was narrow and dark, rising straight up from the hall, with a long landing and rooms leading off. At the far end another, even narrower, flight of steps led up to more attic rooms. Emma opened the first door she came to and went in. The bed was high, covered with a white lace counterpane, and looked so inviting. Tim was right. She was exhausted—but she wasn't going to tell him so.

She crossed the room and gazed through its window. On the opposite side of the narrow road, the sea stretched away to where a line of sinister black rocks jutted from the sloping green coast. A butterfly fluttered dry dusty wings against the glass, and she undid the catch to let it escape into the warm evening air.

Voices drifted up from people strolling past. Emma leaned out to listen. Would one of them be Steve? *What a stupid thing to think*, she told herself. Why should he even be here, in Coverack? But she had seen his name, written only the day before. He had to be somewhere near. And she had to find him.

But with Detective Inspector Tim Goring, so intent on Steve's arrest, which of them would reach him first?

CHAPTER SIX

Later, they walked down the hill to a little café and sat at a wooden table outside, eating crisp fried fish, caught that morning, and thick uneven chips, with peas covering the rest of the wide white plate. Chunks of granary bread filled a wicker basket, while coffee steamed in blue pottery mugs.

'There's home-made apple and gooseberry pie and clotted cream to follow, if you'd like some,' the waitress said, with a smile dimpling her cheeks, as she took away their empty plates.

'Oh, I really couldn't—'

'You could,' Tim said, and ordered.

'I'll burst,' Emma protested, looking in alarm at the huge portion that appeared in front of her.

Tim pushed a bowl of cream across the table. 'Then it's a good job we're sitting outside, isn't it?' he said, his blue eyes filled with humour.

She smiled back at him, watching as he

spooned a large dollop of clotted cream onto the sugary crust of his pie. *What a strange combination we are,* she thought. *Both trying to track down the same man, but for entirely different reasons. And yet, this policeman is such a caring man. To me, he's shown only consideration and kindness.*

But she knew only too well that if he did find Steve, DI Goring would show no mercy at all.

She glanced round at the other people sitting outside the café. A family of four, red from the day's sunshine, with one small child lolling its weary head against the man's shoulder. The other, a little boy, probed an enquiring finger into the mound of pasta on his plate, while his mother quickly pulled a wet-wipe from a packet, and waited in readiness.

At the far side a young couple sat, bodies almost touching. *Probably on honeymoon,* Emma thought, seeing the way they gazed at each other and let their fingers entwine.

And she wondered what people passing by made of her and Tim, eating and laughing together. Did they guess that he was a policeman, and she . . . *What am I?* she asked herself. *A victim—is that how Tim thinks of me? Or maybe a useful witness for when he comes to arrest Steve?*

As they climbed back up the hill, he turned and held out a hand. For a moment she stared at it, not wanting to admit that she found the steepness exhausting but, looking up into his face and seeing the expression of concern, she reached out and felt his fingers curl round hers.

'Not far now,' he said, slowing his pace to match her own.

The setting sun was like a huge ball of fire, slipping below the horizon, but as it vanished it left a deep blaze of colour flooding across the sea, to reflect on the windows of the house when they reached it.

Even though she was tired, Emma lay awake for quite a while. Outside she could hear the drag of waves on shingle; smell salt drifting in through the open window; feel a slight breeze waft over her skin.

There were strange, unusual sounds, too. The faint rattle of steel ropes against the masts of little fishing boats in the harbour close by, as the wind grew stronger. The whoosh from waders and boots of fishermen walking along the stone jetty to set off while the tide was high. And, more familiar, the shriek of gulls making the most of the final strands of daylight, and an occasional car passing below the window.

Downstairs Tim was moving about in the kitchen, closing cupboards and doors. She heard the creak of stairs as he climbed them. Water gushed in the bathroom. The latch of his bedroom door clattered. A light clicked on and, minutes later, off again. Comforting sounds.

Sighing contentedly, she snuggled down under the duvet, but before she quite fell asleep, her thoughts were of Steve. And Alison. And their children. He was somewhere, she knew. Somewhere close by. Maybe, with luck on her side, tomorrow she would find him.

Steve was laughing. Emma could hear it quite loudly. See his handsome face, his open mouth, revealing even white teeth. They were in a church, its pillars rising up to a high vaulted ceiling that echoed with his laughter. He was writing, filling the whole page of a huge book with that swirling S.

She reached out her hand to touch him, but Alison was there in front of her, holding baby Charlotte in her arms, with Mark clutching the skirt of her denim dress.

Steve's laughter grew louder and louder, the noise echoing into Emma's ears. She opened her eyes. Through the open window she could see a grey and white gull, standing on the sea wall, yellow beak wide as it squawked. The tide was out now, leaving dark rocks and a long expanse of sand, strewn with strands of seaweed, where wading birds delved their long beaks. Boats leaned sideways on the mud of the harbour. Sunshine streamed in, filling the room with brilliance.

The smell of bacon caught at her throat

and for a moment she felt her stomach heave, then slowly settle as she breathed deeply. It was morning. Another day. The one when she would find Steve.

*   *   *

'So where would you like to go today, Emma?' Tim was buttering toast, dark head bent, so that a flop of hair fell over his eyes, as he concentrated on the task in hand. 'I am on holiday, don't forget,' he added, licking crumbs from his fingers.

'I thought policemen were never off duty,' Emma commented wryly.

'This one is.'

Emma shook cornflakes into a bowl, and added milk. 'So, if you saw Steve, you'd just ignore him, would you?'

Tim bit into his toast and chewed it while he considered. 'Nope, but I wouldn't rush up and snap on the handcuffs, if that's what you're thinking.'

'What would you do?' she persisted.

'Oh, Emma, must you ask all these questions? Just forget about Steve. Enjoy being down here. Come on, it's a glorious day out there.'

'I want to know.'

He sighed. 'Well, probably I'd follow him. See where he's hanging out. Then contact the local police and my team back home.' He pushed back his chair. 'Are you ready for some toast?'

'Yes, please.' Spooning up the last cornflake, she moved her bowl away. 'And then what would you do?'

'Emma! Be realistic for goodness' sake. You know it's unlikely we'll ever see him. Just eat up that toast and stop worrying.'

But I need to know, she thought, *if I'm to be one jump ahead of you, Detective Inspector Goring.*

Leaning sideways, he tugged a local guidebook from one of the crammed shelves lining the wall, sending half a dozen books cascading onto the floor.

'Look, choose wherever you'd like to go and I'll take you—but let's forget about Steve, for one day at least.'

A sudden wave of nausea swept over her and she breathed deeply, pushing her plate away, pressing her lips together. With his baby growing inside her, how could she ever forget Steve?

'It's okay, Emma. Keep breathing deeply. Come on over to the window. It'll be cooler there.'

Tim's arm was firmly round her waist, as Emma let herself be guided to a wooden chair and leaned back in it, fighting off the desperate feeling.

'Have one of these.'

She made herself look down at his hand and

73

smiled. 'A glacier mint?'

'My sister swore by them when she was pregnant each time. I'm surprised all her babies weren't born like miniature dragons, breathing out fumes of peppermint, she ate so many.'

Carefully she unwrapped the sweet, and put it in her mouth. He waited for a few moments, then raised one eyebrow in question. 'Any better?'

'Surprisingly so,' she admitted, sitting up more comfortably and beginning to relax.

'We'll take the bag with us, just in case.'

'You have a sister?'

'Two. One older and one younger. And a brother.'

'I never thought of you as being part of a family.'

Grinning, he said, 'You thought I'd hatched out from under a stone, did you? Like some evil monster? According to my mother, the stork brought us, but she can't get away telling that tale to her grandchildren. They all seem to know the facts of life before they're even three.'

A sudden thought crossed her mind, remembering when he'd told her about his wife. 'Do you have children?'

His expression changed from laughter to sadness and he shook his head. 'My wife was in the police force, too.'

'I know, you told me,' she said gently. 'And

about what happened to her in the hostage situation.'

Moving back to the table, he began to gather up the plates and bowls. 'We always intended to have a family. She was so good with my sister's four, but we kept putting it off and then—that villain put paid to all that.'

The note in his voice changed, and Emma realised that this was one of the reasons Tim Goring was so intent on catching criminals. And after what had happened to his wife, it wasn't surprising.

But she still refused to think of Steve as a criminal.

'So,' he said, picking up the guidebook, and quickly changing the subject. 'Where are we going, then?'

Sunbeams filtered in through the salt-hazed window, creating tiny rainbows along the rim of a glass of orange juice that Tim had poured for her. All nausea gone and having finished her peppermint, Emma sipped it, savouring the sharp acidity of the liquid.

Tim was right. It was a beautiful day. Steve could be anywhere. So far, everything leading her in his direction had come quite by chance. First, that casual remark by the boy living next door about Alison having a relation in Cornwall. Then going into the church, picking up the fallen pen, and seeing Steve's boldly written name.

All chance happenings. Fate was definitely

on her side. She knew he was in this area. Somewhere close by. They were meant to meet. It was only a matter of time.

Emma drank the rest of the orange juice and smiled at Tim Goring. 'Okay, let's open this at random and go wherever it says.'

'So long as it's not the lighthouse off Land's End. I don't fancy a swim out that far, towing you with me.'

Solemnly he picked up the guidebook and handed it to her. For a moment she gripped it tightly and, closing her eyes, made a silent wish that they'd find Steve there, before letting the pages fall open.

'St Mawes Castle.'

Tim drained the last of his coffee and stood up. 'That's easy enough. Not far, either. We can cross by the King Harry car ferry near Trelissick Gardens. It's quicker than going right up beyond Truro by road. Where's your jacket?'

So is that where I'm going to find Steve? Emma wondered.

CHAPTER SEVEN

The ferry was a low, flat open-ended craft, with high sides, waiting by the water's edge at the bottom of a steep lane. Tim drove on, parked behind a closely packed row of other

76

cars, and switched off the engine.

'This is all part of the Fal estuary, Emma. Falmouth and the Carrick Roads are down that way,' he said, pointing. 'One of the three largest natural harbours in the world. There are lots of little creeks and rivers leading off all the way up.'

Which means a myriad different places where Steve and his family could be, thought Emma. *It really is a hopeless task trying to find them.*

The land was slipping away from them now and she realised the ferry was moving slowly across to where a line of cars already waited on the opposite side of the river. Dense trees covered the hills sloping right down into the water, their lower branches bare and bleached from the salt.

A deeply tanned young man, stripped to the waist and wearing faded denim shorts, leaned in through the car window to take their fare, tucking the ticket into Tim's hand before going on to the next vehicle.

Looking back the way they'd come, Emma could see thick chains below the surface of the water that were taking the ferry across. Already more cars were coming down the hill behind them, ready to board once it completed its return journey.

'You don't have to stay in the car, Emma. Look, there are some steps over there, leading up to a little deck. You'll get a good view of the river in both directions from there.'

'This isn't a ploy to drive off without me when we reach the other side, is it? So that you can continue the search for Steve without me?'

She watched his eyes crinkle at the corners as he grinned. 'As if I would do such a thing.' He leaned across to open the door, and she felt the warmth of his body rest against hers for a moment, her breath catching in her throat. 'Careful how you get out, though. There's not very much room between the cars.'

'I'm not that fat—yet,' she protested, and heard him chuckle.

A light breeze was blowing when she reached the top of the steps and stood, holding onto the rail, with the sun warming her skin, breathing in the mild salt air. Under the trees, further along the far bank, a slight movement caught her gaze Quickly she focused on the grey body of a heron, poised on one leg, beady eye alert as it stared into the water before its long beak was down and back again, the silvery gleam of a fish held there.

Turning her head, she saw a white-sailed yacht drifting across the river towards them and her fingers clenched round the rail, certain the ferry would hit and crush it. But just at the last moment it swung sideways with a flutter of sail, and turned back upstream.

On the deck below, cars were lined up nose to tail. She could see Tim's elbow resting on the open side window, and the dark silhouette of his head. *What is he thinking?* she wondered.

Always on the alert, rather like that heron, poised and waiting, ready to make his catch. And yet, so thoughtful and kind too.

Her gaze wandered on over the vehicles behind him. A small white van with an enormous Cornish pasty standing on top. Next to that was a sleek black open-topped sports car, its driver deeply tanned, drumming his fingers on the steering wheel, obviously impatient to be off and away.

The youth collecting the money had reached the last vehicle, the muscles of his sunburnt back rippling when he bent to pass the ticket through its window before he moved on to the front of the ferry, ready to open the gates when it arrived.

'Why can't I get out and stand up there like that lady, Daddy?' A child's voice drew Emma's gaze to a car in the line directly below her. And she found herself looking at a face she knew well.

Steve's face. A face that now revealed a myriad expressions chasing over it as his shocked eyes stared straight back into her own.

There was a slight jolt as the ferry ground against the bottom of the sloping road where it met the water. Quickly, Emma ran back down the steps, opened the door and climbed back into Tim's car as he started up the engine.

'Thought you weren't going to make it.' Smiling across at her, he eased into gear, letting the car roll forward, following the car in front as it bumped down the ramp and began to climb the narrow winding hill.

She looked sideways at him, seeing the strong thrust of his jaw, the way his eyes were intent on the steep road as it twisted round tight bends. She was aware of grass banks growing high on either side, pink with campion and foxgloves, honeysuckle twining down from the hedges to mingle with them in pale garlands.

All I have to do is tell him, she decided. *And after that . . .*

'Did you have a good view from up there on the top deck?' His voice broke into her thoughts.

'Yes,' she said abruptly, her mind in turmoil.

Steve was in the red estate car only a short distance behind. Steve. The man who had falsely married her and stolen her money. That's what she should be telling Tim. Now.

And Tim would arrest Steve. Right there, in front of his wife and children. She twisted her head round, but her view was blocked by the white van with its Cornish pasty on top.

Tim opened his window a little wider. 'When we reach St Mawes, we'll have coffee and something to eat, shall we? It's hours since breakfast, and I'm really not used to all this fresh air.' He eased the car past a post van parked half-on the grass verge, and grinned at her. 'Spending all my time grilling suspects in dark cells, using bright lights and depriving them of food, until they confess—Emma! Look out!'

The car braked violently, veering sideways, its wheels tearing through the long grass of the verge until it came to a stop just before it reached a half-hidden stone wall. As she started to be flung forward, Emma felt the seatbelt cut across her body, jerking her backwards.

'Maniac!' Tim roared, and she watched as the red estate car raced past. 'Are you all right, Emma?'

For a moment, she couldn't speak. Her palms stung from where they'd hit the dashboard and she was breathless with shock. Easing the seatbelt away from her stomach, she nodded, and rubbed her shoulder.

Restarting the engine, Tim began to back the car off the grass.

'Stop!' she shrieked, twisting round. 'There's something coming.'

'It's okay, I can see it, Emma.'

The low open-topped sports car pulled in behind them and its driver jumped out, red-faced with anger. 'Look what he's done to my Porsche,' he bellowed, waving his hand at a deep scrape along one side. 'Only had it delivered yesterday. Set me back over seventy grand. Didn't catch his number, did you? Creatures like that shouldn't be allowed a licence.'

'Let's move away from this bend before

someone else hits us,' Tim suggested quietly. 'If you pull over into the gateway of that field just along there, I'll give you my details as a witness to the way he was driving.'

While the two men exchanged notes, Emma remained in the car. Her whole body ached from the impact. Everything had happened so fast. It was unbelievable. That was undeniably Steve's car—and he'd deliberately run them off the road.

If it hadn't been for Tim's quick reaction, swerving out of the other car's path, they could both have been killed. She clenched her teeth over her lip, trying to stop it from quivering, but couldn't prevent her mind from racing on, filled with horrific pictures of what might have been.

With a wave to the other driver, Tim climbed in beside her again. 'You should see that poor guy's new car. Needs a new headlight, wing and door. These narrow lanes can be really dangerous, when people drive at ridiculous speeds like that vehicle was doing. Trying to get past on a bend like that one.' He shook his head. 'With children in the car, too. He must be mad.'

'He probably had to be somewhere urgently,' Emma said, guilt pulsing through her, making her voice ragged.

Tim's head turned in her direction, his eyes filled with concern. 'Are you sure you're all right? You look horribly pale.' He edged the

82

car away from the gateway and back out onto the road. 'I'm so sorry, but there was nothing else I could do to get out of his way, when I saw him coming in my side mirror.' He looked at her again, before he put his foot lightly on the accelerator. 'Strong sweet tea is what you need. Another ten minutes and we'll be in St Mawes.'

Emma's fingers clutched at the armrest of the door. 'Please don't drive too fast, will you, Tim?'

His left hand closed over hers for a brief moment, then returned to grip the steering wheel. 'I won't, Emma. I won't.'

St Mawes was a pretty place, with a straggle of shops overlooking the harbour, while a mixture of terraced houses and cottages meandered away from them, on up the hill. Tim stopped in the first empty space of the nearby car park and leaned across to open her door.

'Are you fit to walk?'

'Of course I am,' she snapped, wondering just how steady her legs would be. Her body was still shaking.

'There's a coffee shop in that little arcade over there,' he said, catching hold of her elbow. 'The sooner we get some tea inside you, the better.'

'I'd rather have coffee,' she protested.

'Tea,' he said firmly. 'With plenty of sugar.'

'But—'

'Remember, Emma?' he teased gently, guiding her in through the glass door. 'Never argue with a policeman. Now, sit down, before you keel over.'

She could see his eyes watching her as the cup rattled againt the saucer when she picked it up, trying to sip the liquid before she spilled it.

'Oh, Emma, that incident back there really has shaken you up, hasn't it?'

Blinking back tears, she nodded.

'Would you rather go straight back to Coverack?'

Swiftly, she shook her head. It was far too soon to face another car journey down those twisty little lanes.

'We'll find a seat and sit quietly for a while in the sunshine, shall we?'

'But what about the castle? That's what we've come to see, isn't it?' *And find Steve*, she added inside her head.

He poured more tea into her cup and spooned in sugar. 'Later, if you're up to it. Now drink that. Your colour's coming back a little now. Are you feeling a bit better?'

'Yes,' she lied, shuddering as she drank the hot sweet tea.

Outside, the sun was warm, the air still and soft. Tim put his arm round her shoulders and steered her across the road to where there was an empty bench by the harbour wall.

A yacht with taut white sails leaned

sideways, heading out to sea. Brightly coloured windsurfers winged to and fro over the water, like a flight of dancing butterflies. The Falmouth to St Mawes ferry chugged in, nudging the stone jetty, while a thigh-booted youth jumped down to wind a thick rope round one of the metal posts.

Emma felt strangely tired, her limbs leaden. Voices around her echoed hollowly. Her head ached and her body too, but she didn't mention it to Tim, guessing he'd whisk her off to the nearest hospital for an instant check-up.

It's only a reaction to the near-miss we had this morning, she told herself. *Given time, it will go away, if I just sit and rest here for a while.*

She could hear people's feet flap against the pavement as they walked past, and the rise and fall of their voices, some shrill, some deep. She felt a slight vibration tremble the ground as the ferry-boat's engine rumbled before it moved away from the jetty, the sound dying away into the distance. Her eyes gradually closed to keep out the brightness of the sun.

When she opened them again, it was to warmth and a faint spicy smell that she couldn't quite define. Her neck was stiff and she realised she was resting on Tim's shoulder. Quickly she drew away, embarrassed.

'Ah, you're awake at last. Now I can move again.' She could sense amusement in his tone as he rotated his shoulders.

'What's the time?' she asked drowsily.

'Half-past one.'

'Half-past one! It can't be.'

'Well, it is. You've been asleep for nearly two hours. I was beginning to worry we'd be here all night. Feeling a bit better now?'

She rubbed her eyes and yawned. 'I think so.'

'Lunch, then?'

'Tim! Don't you ever stop eating?'

He stood up and stretched, one hand rubbing the back of his neck. 'It's been a long time since breakfast.'

'But you had a scone at that coffee place.'

He grinned, wrinkling his nose. 'That was over two hours ago and don't forget I've been supporting your weight for all that time. It took a lot of energy. Look, there's a pub over there, just by the bottom of the hill. How about that? Can you get that far?'

Her headache had eased, but her mouth felt very dry. A long, cold drink would be welcome.

'Of course I can. I told you, I'm fine,' she said, but as she began to walk, her legs wobbled. Too long sitting down in one position, she decided, and was glad the pub was close by.

Inside it was cool and airy. Low-ceilinged, with dark wooden beams. Tim guided her to a corner by a door that opened onto a courtyard, where large terracotta pots filled with petunias, lobelia, begonias and fuchsia created patches of bright colour. Thankfully,

Emma sank onto a cushioned wooden bench. Even the short walk across from the harbour had exhausted her.

'I'm not very hungry,' she said, as the waitress handed them menus, and all the time her mind was repeating the same question over and over again. *Why haven't I told Tim who was driving that car?*

'How about a salad then?' she heard Tim ask. 'The smoked mackerel is always good here.'

'Just something long and iced to drink will do.'

*   *   *

The drive back was uneventful. At first, Emma clung to the door handle, ready to leap out at the slightest sign of danger, but she needn't have worried. Tim drove very carefully, fully aware of her nervousness.

While they waited in a queue of cars for the ferry to arrive, she watched its ponderous progress across the narrow stretch of fast-flowing water, seeing sunshine glint on the windows and roofs of vehicles lined up on its deck. Her own skin glowed with warmth from the time she'd spent asleep in the sun earlier by the harbour.

Glancing sideways from under her lashes, she studied Tim's profile. The dark hair, ruffled by a day in the wind, the broad forehead, thick arched eyebrows above those blue eyes that seemed to constantly change their depth of colour, sometimes a deep azure sometimes almost grey, and sometimes sharp as steel. His nose, she decided, wasn't classically straight. It had a slight bump in the middle and she wondered whether he had broken it in the past.

But it was his mouth that intrigued her most— fairly wide, curving upwards at the corners when he smiled, but set in a firm line when he was angry. Not that she'd seen that happen very often.

She was still gazing thoughtfully at his lips, when she realised that his head had turned towards her. For one long moment, his gaze held hers, making her breath catch in her throat.

The noise of engines revving, as vehicles prepared to leave the ferry, broke the spell.

Tim brushed away a leaf that had blown in through the open window onto his shoulder. 'Would you like to visit Trelissick Gardens on the way home? We pass right by the gates and they do good cream teas.'

She shook her head. 'It sounds very tempting, but I'd rather get back. A long soak in the bath might ease these aches.'

His eyes were dark with worry when he looked at her. 'You're not feeling too good?' he asked.

'Only a bit of backache. I think I must have

jarred it. Probably when the seatbelt stopped me from hitting the windscreen.' *And a guilty conscience*, she thought.

'Why didn't you say, Emma? We could have come home sooner.'

'Don't worry so, Tim. I'm fine. Nothing a hot bath won't cure. I've ruined your day enough as it is, sleeping for so long on that seat. Making you miss seeing the castle.'

'There'll always be another time.' His eyebrows drew together in a slight frown. 'You didn't have too much sun, did you?'

She laughed, holding her painful ribs as she did so. 'No, but from the look of your nose, you did.'

Ahead of them, the cars started to move forward, and Tim followed the queue smoothly onto the ferry.

'I've enjoyed today, Tim,' she declared, watching the land slip away once more as it moved off.

'Despite what happened?'

'Without your skilful driving, it could have been disastrous for us both.'

'All part of the training in my job, Emma.'

His words startled her. For a little while, she'd quite forgotten that he was a policeman.

*   *   *

Water gushed into the bath, hot and steamy. There was a bottle of gel on the shelf and she poured in a capful of the blue liquid. Sinking into the fragrant bubbles, she let herself relax, hoping the dull pain in her back would ease. There was a red weal from her shoulder right down and across her stomach, where the seatbelt had caught and held her. Without that, she shuddered to think what might have happened. But Tim's reaction had been so rapid. Instinctive. Part of his police training, he'd said.

And now it was Tim who filled her thoughts. Not Steve, the man who had deliberately caused that accident, but Tim, whose company she'd enjoyed all day. Tim, with his humour, his caring and his kindness.

Somehow she couldn't see Steve sitting in all that heat, keeping quite still for hours while she slept, sheltering her from the sun with his body.

She closed her eyes, letting herself sink further into the warm water. The pain in her back wasn't easing. It was growing worse, encircling her in a band of increasing agony.

As another intense wave stabbed through her, suddenly she knew what was happening.

She was losing her baby.

CHAPTER EIGHT

The small room at the hospital held beds for two patients. Only one was occupied— Emma's.

But from along the corridor, she could hear the wail of babies. It seemed too cruel. When she woke, it was still evening, yet she felt sure there must have been a day somewhere in between. Maybe they'd sedated her. She couldn't remember.

Her whole body felt as though she'd been beaten, every bone and muscle aching. Cautiously, she slid her hand down over the curve of her stomach—and then she knew for certain.

A figure was sitting by the side of her bed. She lifted her head from the mound of pillows and saw it was Tim, sleeping, hunched in a high-backed chair. His dark hair was tousled, his chin shadowed with stubble. She'd never realised what thick eyelashes he had. Or that his mouth curved upwards, even in sleep.

Far too thin and angular for it to be called a handsome face. Not like Steve's good looks. But what did appearance matter, when the character beneath was such an attractive and endearing one?

His whole body was slumped, like a puppet with broken strings. He looked utterly exhausted, lines etched deep across his cheeks. A man who constantly lived by his wits, always having to be one jump ahead of any villain he encountered.

And Steve was a villain. Tim was quite right about that. So had he really tried to kill her? Emma remembered the look of horror filling his expression when he'd seen her on the ferry. But what on earth made him run them off the road like that, risking the lives of his wife and children at the same time? He couldn't know that Tim Goring was a policeman, or that he was searching for him. Was it just that he panicked after seeing her and was trying to escape by getting ahead of them on the road?

Her mouth felt dry. She was desperately thirsty. Cautiously, she raised herself on one elbow and reached towards a plastic jug of water on the bedside cabinet. As she held it over a beaker, the lid fell off with a clatter of sound, and landed on the floor.

Tim shot up in his chair, whole body instantly alert.

'Sorry!' she whispered.

'Emma! You're awake. How are you feeling now?' His eyes filled with sadness as he continued. 'I'm so very sorry about the baby.'

Her hand shook as she poured water into the beaker, spilling some on the sheet. When she spoke, the words came out in a gabble. 'It's for the best. It wouldn't have worked out. I'd never have coped on my own. I was being stupid to even think I could.' But then her tears brimmed over to cascade down her cheeks, and there was nothing she could do to stop them.

'Oh, Emma, Emma, my poor darling.' Tim's arms closed round her and she buried her face into the soft fabric of his sweatshirt, while his fingers smoothed the nape of her neck in soothing circles.

'Cry as much as you like, Emma.' His voice was gentle in her ear, his lips lightly brushing it like a butterfly's wing. 'It might help a little to ease away some of your grief.'

'I'm sorry,' she sobbed. 'I just can't help it.'

His hand touched her cheek. 'You've been through so much. Of course you can't. All your emotions are churned up. You're bound to feel like this.'

She stayed there, with his arms holding her, for a long time. Long after she'd stopped crying. There wasn't any reason to move away.

A nurse came in later, bringing a couple of tablets for her to take and to tuck the covers firmly round her. She smiled across at Tim. 'I'm afraid your partner will have to leave now, Ms Taylor. He can come back tomorrow. Visiting hours are from two o'clock onwards.'

Emma struggled against the tight bedclothes to sit upright. 'But I'm perfectly all right now, so there's nothing to prevent me from going home.'

The nurse smiled again. 'Sorry, Ms Taylor.

I'm afraid you'll have to wait until the doctors do their round tomorrow before we can make any decision. A good night's sleep and you'll be feeling a lot better.'

'But I am feeling a lot better,' Emma insisted.

'Tomorrow, Ms Taylor,' the nurse said firmly.

'Tim! Please. Tell her I'm all right.'

He bent and kissed the top of her head. 'Tomorrow, Emma. Wait until tomorrow. It's for the best. I'll be back then.'

The pills were taking effect. Emma realised she couldn't fight any more. Sinking into the pillows, she drifted away. But just before sleep overtook her completely, she smiled drowsily. That nurse had believed Tim was her partner. And he had kissed her.

*   *   *

At first she thought it was those annoying seagulls shrieking. Then, when she woke properly, she realised it was the wail of babies. But not her baby. Her baby would never cry. All she would ever have was a memory of what might have been.

Someone else was sleeping in the bed opposite now. Emma could just make out a thick straggle of curly hair over the pillows. Out in the corridor a trolley rattled along, then stopped and a face peered round the door.

'Tea or coffee, ladies?'

'Tea, please,' Emma said, sitting up, relieved to find that the pain in her body had dulled a little. 'No sugar.'

'What about the other lady?'

The woman in the opposite bed slowly emerged from the covers, yawning as she pushed back the thick curls almost hiding her face. Emma stared, not believing who she was seeing.

It was Steve's wife. Alison. Fate had struck yet again.

'Oh, tea for me too, please. Milk and two sugars.' Alison yawned again, before her gaze eventually focussed on Emma. 'Oh, hi, I'm Alison Jones.'

'Emma Taylor,' Emma said, taking a mug from the tea-lady and wrapping her hands round its warmth.

Any further conversation came to an abrupt end when two nurses came in to change the sheets and re-make their beds.

'Are you all right to wash on your own, Ms Taylor, or do you need some help?' one of them asked Emma.

'Of course I can wash myself.'

'Just asking, that's all. Use the basin in here. There's a bathroom down the corridor, on the left, but you'd better wait until someone can come with you, if you want a bath or shower.'

'Why? I'm perfectly capable of showering.'

'Rules. You might feel faint. You lost quite

95

a lot of blood. Press the buzzer by your bed if you need anyone.' And they both went out.

Alison looked across at Emma in concern. 'Oh—you haven't had a miscarriage, have you?'

Emma nodded. 'And you . . .?' The question dwindled away.

'No, my blood pressure's rocketed up, that's all. Doctor decided I needed to be checked out. Not surprising with all the rushing around my Steve's been making me and the kids do. Suddenly decided we'd take a holiday, just like that, right out of the blue, and off we had to go.'

'You're on holiday down here? Are you staying in Falmouth?' Emma asked, trying to keep her voice casual.

'No, with my aunt. She lives out on the Lizard Only been there for a few days when all this blew up.' Alison reached sideways to put her cup and saucer on the bedside locker. 'But we nearly had a car crash yesterday. Don't think that helped. Really scared me, it did.' She frowned and her teeth bit into her lower lip. 'How my Steve's coping with Charlotte—that's my little girl—I dread to think. She's at that clinging stage. Can't bear me out of her sight. He'll have his hands full, I can tell you.'

Emma took a gulp of tea. 'He'll be in later to see you, then?'

'He'd better be! I need a change of nightie. Promised he'd be in after lunch, when he's been to Marks & Sparks for one. Hope he remembers to get cotton. I can't bear any of those man-made fibres—they make you really hot and itchy, don't they?'

'I need a few things, too.' Emma said, putting the empty cup back onto its saucer. 'I wonder whether there's a phone anywhere I can use. That notice says mobiles aren't permitted.'

'Sure to be one down the corridor. Are you allowed out of bed, though?'

'No one's told me not to. That nurse just said I wasn't to bath or shower on my own.'

'Here, you'd better borrow my dressing-gown. That hospital thing only does up with tapes at the back and it's not really covering you very well.'

'Thanks.' Emma smiled at her as she slipped into the cotton housecoat and immediately felt guilty.

Her intention was to phone Tim Goring and tell him Steve would be right here, in the hospital, that afternoon. But now she was hesitating. Would it be fair to Alison? Or her children? Who would look after them, with Alison in hospital, if Steve was arrested? Charlotte was going through a clingy phase, Alison said. Could the aunt cope? The poor child had probably never even seen her before and, with her mother not there, only her father who was absent for most of her life, what effect would it have on such a baby? And as for the little boy, Mark—at three, he wasn't old enough to understand why his mother wasn't with them.

Once she was outside the door, Emma could see a wall-phone at the end of the corridor. She'd decided what she would do. Phone Tim and tell him not to come in that afternoon. Say she felt too poorly to see anyone. She had to make him stay away. Stop him from meeting Steve.

Emma couldn't be sure what Steve's reaction would be when he saw her again, and at the same hospital as his wife, but she guessed that he'd try to get as far away as possible.

'Ms Taylor!' An indignant voice boomed out from behind her. Startled, Emma swung round. A tall, broadly-built nurse was hurrying down the corridor towards her, the rubber soles of her flat black shoes squeaking as she walked. 'And where do you think you're going?'

'I need to make a phone call.'

'Back into bed this instant. The doctors haven't done their rounds yet this morning, and until they do, you stay there. Then, and only then, will we decide what happens to you.'

'And if I discharge myself?' Emma asked defiantly.

'After the amount of blood you've just lost, you'd be a very silly young lady,' she retorted, taking her by the arm. 'Now, back into that bed.'

Feeling like a naughty schoolgirl, Emma obeyed, and the sheets were tucked in tightly again.

'I'll have one of the nurses bring you in a trolley phone if it's so urgent.'

On the other side of the room, Alison put down the magazine she was reading. 'I can always ask my Steve to get you anything you want,' she offered kindly. 'There's a League of Friends' shop on the ground floor. They're usually pretty good for odds and ends you've come without.'

But not for getting an urgent message to DI Goring, Emma thought. She could hear the trundle of wheels coming down the corridor and looked up to see a little Asian nurse backing in through the door with a trolley-phone. Eagerly, she sat up, ready to make the call.

'Can you wait a minute while I do your Obs first?' the nurse asked, twisting the cuff of a manometer round Emma's arm. 'Just need to check your blood pressure. Staff Nurse said you seemed a bit agitated. I'll do your temperature as well.' She glanced across the room. 'Won't be more than a couple of minutes with Ms Taylor, then I'll be over to do yours, Mrs Jones.'

Emma leaned back against the pillows, breathing deeply, trying to keep calm while the readings were taken. It was nearly twelve o'clock. Only two hours before visiting began. She had to stop Tim Goring getting there, and seeing Steve.

'There now, Ms Taylor. All done.' The nurse was releasing the cuff. 'Right, Mrs Jones. Your turn now.'

With Alison distracted, Emma pulled the trolley-phone closer, delving one hand into her bag to find her diary with Tim's number—and then realised that the only one she had was for the police station back home. That was the number she'd used to make the call, after she discovered Steve's name in the church visitors' book.

Whoever she'd spoken to then had contacted Tim on his mobile phone—and she didn't have that number. There was no way she could contact him and stop him from arriving. And when he did . . .

She looked across at Alison. Steve would be there in a couple of hours. So would Tim. When they met, Alison's life would never be the same again.

*   *   *

Emma watched the digital numbers of the wall clock change. Twelve twenty-five. She couldn't believe how quickly the time was passing. Lunch was brought in, but she wasn't hungry and pushed the tray to the back of the bed-table.

Alison seemed to be enjoying hers, blissfully ignorant of what was about happen. She smiled across at Emma.

'You really should eat, you know. Need to build yourself up. I had a miscarriage before I got pregnant with Mark. Pulls you down a bit. Still, you're only young, aren't you? Plenty of time to catch up. Hubby coming in later?'

'I'm not married.'

'Oh. Sorry. Shouldn't jump to conclusions like that, should I?'

'How was your blood pressure? Any better?' Emma said, quickly changing the subject.

Alison screwed up her face ruefully. 'Still much too high. Got to keep calm and hope it goes down. Could be a problem if it doesn't. I don't want to lose this baby.' She broke off, looking embarrassed. 'Oh, Emma, I'm so sorry. I just didn't think.'

So what effect will her husband being arrested have on her? Emma asked herself. *How calm will she be then?*

Twelve forty-five. Just over an hour and Tim would be there, only then he'd become Detective Inspector Goring. Emma sank her head into her hands, pressing them against her aching forehead, trying to think what to do. The trolley-phone was still by her bed. There was still time to phone the police station back home. Either get them to contact Tim on his mobile, or ask for the number herself. But would they give it to her? Probably not, for security reasons.

She looked at the phone, then across at Alison. There was no way she could make the call, without her hearing every word, and she'd be bound to ask Emma why she was speaking to the police.

Thirteen fifty-five. The lunch trays were cleared away. Beds tidied by the nurses. Any moment now feet would come clattering down the corridor, the door would open and Steve, or maybe Tim Goring, would be first in.

But then, to Emma's complete amazement, fate took a hand once more. One of the nurses popped her head round the door. 'Ms Taylor, there's a message for you. From a Tim Goring. Says he's going to be a bit late. Punctured a car tyre on his way here, Probably be another half hour or so 'til he gets here, he reckons.'

'Tim? Is that your boyfriend?' Alison asked, eyebrow raised.

'Just a friend,' Emma replied, and paused for a moment before continuing more slowly. 'I was in his car when we had the accident. We'd just driven off the King Harry ferry. Tim had to swerve sharply onto the grass verge to avoid a car that came racing past at high speed, and almost hit the stone wall.'

'The King Harry ferry?' Alison looked startled. 'Is that what caused you to lose the baby?'

'Um. Probably. Yes.'

'Was it this man's baby?'

Emma shook her head. 'Not Tim's, no.'

Her thoughts were racing. Half an hour or so. It meant that Tim could still meet up with Steve, but would he recognise him? *If I don't say anything, Emma decided, he might not. After all, he's only seen a photograph.*

She could hear footsteps on the polished floor of the corridor outside. The door swung open. Quickly, she slid down under the bed covers and pulled them close to her face.

'Steve!' The happiness in Alison's voice pierced through Emma. 'I thought you'd never come. How's Charlie? Did you make sure she had her comfort-blanket before you left her with Aunty? And Mark? Have you remembered to put plenty of sun-cream on him when he's out in Aunty's garden and on the beach?'

'Of course I have, love. Don't get so worked up about everything. You know what the doctor said. You've got to stay calm.'

Emma listened, hearing the soothing note in his voice and the gentle way he spoke to his wife. This was the woman he loved—not her.

So why did he marry her?

And then she remembered bitterly. Fifty thousand pounds. That was the reason. Tim Goring was right. Steve was a criminal. But even so, he didn't deserve prison—and that was where Inspector Goring was determined that he'd end up.

'Oh, Steve!' Emma heard Alison's voice

continuing. 'I said cotton. You know how I hate man-made fibres. Especially when I've got to lie in bed for days on end.'

'Okay, love, don't get upset. You know what it'll do to your blood pressure. I've got the receipt. I'll take them back and change them. Bring them in this evening.'

'You'd better leave it until tomorrow, Steve. By the time you've bathed the kids and settled Charlie, and read Mark his stories, visiting hours will almost be over.' Alison sighed in frustration. 'I'll just have to wear this grubby one until then, I suppose.'

'Tell you what, love. If I pop off to M&S now, I can drop them in at Reception later this afternoon and ask someone to bring them up to you. You'll feel better in a nice clean nightie.'

'Oh, would you, Steve? You're such a darling.'

Remaining hidden under the covers, Emma heard a chair scrape on the floor, then the sound of a kiss. By slightly lifting her head, she could see the clock. Fourteen twenty-two. Any minute now, Tim would arrive. Her fingers curled into her palms, as she waited tensely.

'Bye, love.' Rapid footsteps began to cross to the door, about to pass the end of her bed.

'Sshh! Don't wake her, Steve. Poor girl. She's just lost her baby.' Alison's voice stilled for a moment. 'She said the car she was in was run off the road, after it came off the ferry.

Oh, Steve, I think it was that car you nearly hit when we came up the hill.'

Emma's body froze as the footsteps ceased right next to her. She felt the bed creak slightly as a weight leaned against it, and heard Steve whisper, 'Lost her baby? No, love. Can't be that girl. Must be a coincidence.'

'Ooh, that's a relief. Look, you'd better hurry, Steve, or you'll never get into town and back.'

He had only been gone a minute or two before Tim Goring rushed in through the door, carrying a bunch of freesias in one hand and bag of fruit in the other, and hesitated by Emma's bed.

Cautiously, Emma pushed back the covers and raised her tousled head.

'Did I wake you?'

'Not really. Just sort of dozing.'

'I'm sorry to be so late. Did you get my message?'

Emma nodded.

'I'd only done a couple of miles, when I realised one of the tyres was flat. Probably weakened on the inside rim when I hit that grass verge, and today it eventually split. Had to stop and change it, and the spare was low on pressure so I had to find a garage and pump it up a bit more.' His mouth twisted sideways. 'Should keep a foot-pump in the boot, but it's in my garage at home.'

He looked round the room. 'Is there

105

anything to put these flowers in? It was so hot in the car that they're starting to droop a bit. And I wasn't sure what sort of fruit you'd like, so I bought one of everything.'

'There's a vase on that windowsill over there, and you can use water from Emma's jug,' Alison called across to them, and Emma realised she was listening to everything they said.

'Thanks,' Tim replied, glancing over at her as he went to fetch it.

'They're lovely,' Emma said, breathing in the freesias' soft scent when he placed the vase on the bedside cabinet. 'My favourite flowers. Thanks, Tim.'

'Is there any news of when you'll be out of here?'

'Not until the doctors do their round, apparently. I feel fine, though. A bit weak, but I suppose that's to be expected after—what happened.'

Tim's hand rested on hers, his thumb stroking it gently.

Looking up at him, her forehead puckered. 'I must have given you an awful shock. Crying out like that in the bath. But you were so calm, wrapping me up in that huge towel, and then the duvet, and talking to me until the ambulance arrived. I don't remember much after that, until I woke up here.'

'Probably best that you don't, Emma,' he said quietly, lifting a curl of hair away from her cheek. 'But you're going to have to rest up for a bit once you're discharged from here and back in Coverack. I just hope it's not tomorrow, though.'

'Why?' she asked. 'I can't wait to leave.'

'I had a phone call earlier this morning.' His mouth turned down ruefully at the corners. 'I'm needed in court tomorrow. There's no way I can avoid it. But it's an open and shut case. Shouldn't take long. I could be here late in the evening, or early the following day.'

'Oh, Tim!' She hated to think of him driving through the night.

'I promise I'll return as quickly as I can, Emma.' Leaning forward, he whispered in her ear. 'And, don't worry, I haven't forgotten about Steve.'

Emma lowered her eyes, knowing what she should tell him, but seeing Alison in the opposite bed, contentedly reading a magazine, and the effect it would have on her and her children, she couldn't let herself do so.

'What time do you have to leave Falmouth tonight, Tim?' she asked.

'I've got my overnight bag in the car. I'll get caught up in the rush hour by the time I reach Exeter in any case, so it'll take five or six hours at least.'

'Then you'd better start now. Oh—and let me have your mobile number so I can keep in touch.'

She watched him scribble something on a

page torn from his notebook and tuck it under the vase of freesias.

'Drive carefully, Tim.'

His fingers curved under her chin and she thought, for a moment, that he was going to kiss her as his head bent towards hers, but he suddenly jerked upright again, and his hand slipped away.

'I'll be back as soon as I can, Emma. I promise. Take care.'

Tears blurred her eyes as she watched him walk quickly towards the door, then turn briefly with an expression on his face that she couldn't read, and was gone.

'He looks a nice sort of guy,' Alison commented.

Emma swallowed the lump in her throat before she could reply. 'Yes,' she agreed. 'He is. A very nice guy.'

But she wondered whether Alison would think the same if she knew that Tim Goring was a policeman—just waiting for the right moment to arrest her husband and put him in prison.

CHAPTER NINE

A tramp of feet came marching along the corridor outside and the door swung open for an army of white-coated figures to sweep into the room, led by an immaculately dark-suited, sleek-haired gentleman. The team of doctors had arrived.

'Curtains!' The command was rapped out and Emma found her bed swiftly enclosed ready for the examination to begin. She shut her eyes as cool fingers started to probe.

'Hmm. All seems to be progressing satisfactorily. Pain anywhere?'

Emma shook her head.

The consultant tugged her gown down again and studied her notes. 'If everything continues to do well, I can see no reason why you shouldn't be discharged, say, the day after tomorrow. There's sure to be a queue waiting for this bed.'

The curtains swished as he and his team stepped through and Emma saw him move across to Alison before she, too, was hidden from sight.

The day after tomorrow. Tim would be back by then. Emma slid down into her pillows, the soft fragrance of the freesias drifting round her. Tomorrow she would find a way to confront Steve—but now she had an overwhelming need to sleep.

He was standing at the end of her bed, looking down at her, one arm holding Alison close to his side. Baby Charlotte snuggled into his shoulder, sucking her thumb, while Mark leaned against his knee. The perfect family group, posed as if for a photograph, Emma thought.

But as she watched, thin curtains of gossamer like a spider's web began to close round her bed, wrapping them up in its folds until they were separated from each other. She saw the children struggle in panic and Alison's mouth open in a silent scream, as Steve's body slowly vanished, leaving a pile of coins that grew higher and higher, until finally they spilled over and she felt the weight of them begin to crush her.

Her eyes flew open in terror, her body tense as she tried to push away their heaviness.

'It's all right, Ms Taylor. Just tucking in your covers a bit more tightly. Visitors will be arriving in five minutes. Need to have you neat and tidy.'

Slowly Emma relaxed, her heartbeat steadying, as the nurse fussed round her. Alison was already sifting stiffly upright against a pile of smooth pillows.

'Thought you must have been having a nightmare, Emma, from all the strange noises you were making, and the way your feet kept kicking about like that. Are you all right?'

Emma tried to smile, the unpleasant dream still hovering round her.

'Is that nice boyfriend of yours coming to see you this evening?'

'No, he's been called back to work.'

'Oh, Emma, you must be disappointed. It's the same problem with my Steve. Never know

110

when he's going to be called out, any time of the day or night. Often away for days on end. Steve's an insurance assessor, you see. What job does your boyfriend do?'

Emma hesitated, but while she was rapidly trying to think up how to answer, the door swung open and Steve hurried in.

'Steve! Alison's voice was full of happiness. 'I didn't think you'd be able to come in tonight, what with Charlie and Mark to put to bed.'

'Your Aunty insisted she could manage, love, so here I am,' he said, bending to kiss her. 'Are those new nighties all right?'

'Lovely, Steve, and so pretty, too, aren't they, Emma?'

Steve's head slowly turned, and Emma watched the range of expressions that flickered across his face when he recognised her. Amazement. Horror. Anxiety. Even fear.

Alison's voice lowered, but Emma could hear quite clearly as she whispered, 'Poor girl. Just think about how we would feel, Steve, if we lost this little one.'

There was a thump against the door and a porter backed his way in, dragging a wheelchair. 'Mrs Jones?'

Alison gave him a startled look. 'Yes?'

'There's a machine vacant just now. They want to see you downstairs for your scan.'

'What—now? Visiting time?' Steve growled.

The man shrugged. 'Told to fetch her, that's all.'

With a sigh, Alison lowered herself over the side of the bed and was wheeled away. Emma breathed in deeply before she looked across to where Steve sat hunched, and said softly, 'Why, Steve?'

He got up from the chair and came to stand glaring down at her. 'Why? I'll tell you why, Emma. I was made redundant over eighteen months ago. I haven't worked since then. Not that I haven't tried.'

He laughed bitterly. 'Oh, my job as an insurance assessor was a complete fabrication. I couldn't let Alison know that, though, could I?' His mouth tightened. 'Our house was about to be repossessed. Everything was going to come crashing round my ears. And then by some strange stroke of chance, I met you.'

Emma waited, her gaze never leaving his face.

'Little innocent Emma, telling all your friends in the pub about the money your grandmother had left you, and how, once probate was granted, it would be about fifty thousand pounds. Fifty thousand pounds! What did a girl like you need with a sum like that?'

'I had my whole life ahead of me,' Emma replied quietly.

'So did I!' Steve roared. 'And the lives of my wife and children. Four, soon to be five of us now, against one. Rather unfair, don't you think, when you weigh up the odds, Emma?'

'Why didn't you tell Alison you'd lost your job? It's quite obvious that she loves you so much, Steve. I'm sure she would have understood.'

'Knowing she loves, and depends on me, is why I couldn't tell her. That we were losing our home. That I was a failure.' His lips twisted. 'That I'd lied about my job. I hated deceiving her, Emma, but once I'd begun, it snowballed and there was no turning back.'

'But marrying me?'

He laughed. 'It was marriage or nothing. You aren't the sort of girl who would settle for anything else, are you? And I needed to make absolutely sure of that money.' He moved closer to her bed. 'So what exactly are you going to do about it, Emma? Hand me over to the police?' His expression sharpened and she saw the fear that sprang into his eyes.

'Or have you already told them I was here, after you saw me this afternoon? Are they waiting outside to arrest me when I leave?'

She answered quietly. 'No one will be waiting, Steve. Not yet, anyway.'

He leaned forward, his hands gripping the rail at the end of her bed.

'Emma, for the sake of Alison and the kids, I'm pleading with you not to say anything. I know it was a terrible thing that I did to you, but really I had no choice, can you see?'

'Of course you had a choice, Steve. You're not the only person this has happened to.

There are people out there who can advise and give help. You didn't have to become a bigamist or a criminal.'

'Please, Emma, give me one more chance. Alison's aunt owns a guest house out on the Lizard. She's getting older now, her knees give her trouble and it's starting to get a bit too much for her. She's asked us whether we'd consider staying on here to help her run it— and in return, she's planning to pay off all my debts.'

Hope shone in his eyes as he pictured his future.

'It would be a fantastic place to bring up our kids, Emma. A new start for us all.' He gave her a searching look. 'But now it depends on you.'

She met his eyes coolly. 'And what about my money, Steve? My inheritance. That fifty thousand pounds you pocketed and ran off with. Remember?'

'I've opened an account with a bank in Falmouth. The money's deposited there.' He was silent for a moment, before he spoke again. 'If you'll agree that Alison never knows about any of this, I'll let you have it back.'

'I don't think you're in any position to bargain with me, Steve.'

'I'll bring you a cheque for the whole amount tomorrow.'

'Oh no, Steve—I don't trust you not to cancel it before I can pay it in. I'll have a

114

banker's draft for that amount tomorrow, thank you very much, before I agree to anything.'

'Will you still be here tomorrow?'

'I'll make sure I am—either as a patient, or back visiting Alison. There's quite a story I could tell her.'

CHAPTER TEN

By the following day, Emma was feeling much stronger and was allowed to sit up in a chair, and finally walk down the corridor to shower in the bathroom. She was in the chair next to Alison's bed when Steve arrived at visiting time. Seeing them talking together, his eyes narrowed and he gave Emma a searching glance.

'Hi, Steve,' she said evenly, getting up.

Silently he handed her a magazine.

Alison beamed at him. 'Ooh, Steve, that was really thoughtful of you.'

Opening it, Emma saw the envelope inside and smiled. 'Thanks, Steve, I'll take it into the sun-lounge to read and leave you two lovebirds alone.'

Her legs were shaking when she reached the room and she sank onto a deep cushioned seat under the long window, with a view down into the hospital grounds. *Tim need never know*, she told herself, but the thought of deceiving him troubled her.

Meeting Steve again, she'd been amazed at her total lack of feeling. The overwhelming love she'd once felt for him was gone. He could have been a complete stranger. And she could see, also, how much Alison and his children meant to him. *So how could he have done such a terrible thing?* Emma wondered. *He must have been quite desperate. No job. About to lose his home. Maybe having his family split up.*

And fate stepped in—to provide him with me. A silly, impressionable young girl about to receive a fortune. No wonder he took such a chance.

Feeling almost guilty about accepting it, Emma slid the banker's draft from its envelope and studied it carefully. Fifty thousand pounds. At least Alison would keep her husband and children together as a family, and never know what he had done.

Steve was gone by the time Emma returned to the room, and Alison was reading a paperback he'd brought her.

'We're not going back to Epsom,' she told Emma excitedly. 'We're going to move in with my aunty and help run the guesthouse for her. I'm her only relative, you see, and she thinks my Steve's a real charmer. She's already told us it'll be ours when she's passed on. He reckons, once he takes over, it'll be a little gold mine. Worth a fortune, he says.'

Emma bent her head, trying not to smile.

*   *   *

She was waiting in the sun-room the next afternoon as the clock clicked minutes into hours. Earlier that morning she'd officially been discharged, and already another patient was in her bed, discussing medical problems across the room with Alison.

When the door opened, Emma looked up quickly, but it was only a nurse with a large bag of medication for her.

'You are being collected by someone, aren't you, Ms Taylor? If not, you can phone through for a taxi.'

'He should be here any time now,' Emma told her. 'It's a long drive.'

Every footstep that passed down the corridor had her rising to her feet. By five o'clock, she was chewing her lip anxiously. There'd been no phone call from Tim. If he didn't arrive soon, she'd have to make her own way back to Coverack.

Eighteen forty-five. The evening visitors would be arriving soon, and that meant Steve would be back. Emma picked up her bag and moved towards the corridor, needing to meet, and stop, Tim before he came into the hospital and saw him. But before she reached there, the door swung open and he came through, sending her heartbeat racing.

117

'Emma!' he breathed, and his cheek was warm against hers as he held her close. She could feel the slight stubble on his chin prickle her skin and his lashes brush her closed eyelids, before he moved away to look deep into her eyes. 'I've missed you so much.'

Back in the car, he settled a soft cushion behind her back and carefully did up her safety belt.

'Tim,' she warned. 'I'm not an invalid.'

'The nurse said you have to take things gently and get plenty of rest.'

'But not that I have to be wrapped up in cotton wool,' she protested.

His smile sent a tremor pulsing through her body. 'Emma, never —'

'I know, I know! Never argue with a policeman.' She leaned her head back against the seat. 'Oh, I'm so glad to be out of there.'

'And so am I. Now we really can turn this into a proper holiday. You can laze on the beach, while I swim, or maybe try surfing.'

'That sounds very chauvinistic, Detective Inspector Goring.' As soon as she'd said them, Emma regretted those last words. Reminding herself once again that Tim was a policeman, and what he was in Cornwall to do.

As he steered the car out through the gates, he said, 'There was no more news of Steve Jones when I got back to the station.'

Emma tried to make her voice sound casual. 'Wasn't there?'

'Could be anywhere in the country by now, of course.'

'Yes, I suppose he could,' she replied carefully, staring out of the window rather than meet his eyes. 'Tim, please can we stop off at the bank in the town? I've realised I need to check whether my account has been transferred to the main branch at home. The old branch was closed down, you know.'

'And you really have to do this right now, today?' he asked, surprised.

'Yes, now. After all that's happened, I want to make sure that I still do have an account.'

'It's all no parking, with double lines, so I'll have to drop you off, then drive round the block and pick you up again. Wouldn't do to be caught by the local police for unlawful parking, would it?' Tim said, with a grin, as he stopped the car.

With the banker's draft safely tucked in her bag, Emma climbed out.

*   *   *

Trees arched the lane they were travelling, making a leafy tunnel, with sunlight flickering through to pattern the road. Its banks were thick with waving feathers of long grass and a confusion of colours where wild flowers grew. Somewhere, in the distance, Emma could hear the sea. And then they were travelling down the steep hill that twisted sharply, first one

119

way, then the other, until the view opened up to reveal the wide bay, bordered by fields that reached down to the rocks.

Parking the car on the scrap of land beside the house, Tim went to unlock the front door, then came back to help her out.

'Tim! I can walk, you know.' But she didn't move away, or dislodge his arm that encircled her waist when he guided her indoors.

The days that followed were a balm for Emma. Days full of sunshine, and happiness she hadn't felt for many months. Tim took her to quiet coves, where they picnicked and she lay on the sand, watching while he swam.

His body was lean but strong, his arms cutting easily through the waves with firm strokes. Each time he emerged, running up the beach on long tanned legs, hair dark and sleek like a seal, scattering sand and seawater, to pick up his towel, Emma's heartbeat quickened. And when he flopped down to stretch out beside her in the sunshine, it was torment.

'Only two more days,' he said, resting on his elbows to look down at her.

The deep tan of his skin made his eyes an even darker blue and his teeth gleam white. She watched the words form on his lips and the way his mouth moved. Smelt the salt on his skin and felt the glow of its warmth. A bead of water meandered slowly from his wet hair to his cheekbone, down to the curve of his chin, and on to the long column of his neck. Emma closed her eyes, shutting out the image of him.

Two more days. After that, they would never meet again. He would be Detective Inspector Goring. And she would return to her old job and the flat she'd once shared with Steve.

*   *   *

Metal ropes frantically rattling against the masts of the little fishing boats in the harbour woke Emma early the next morning. Huge, white-crested waves were roaring in across the bay to crash over the rocks, sending up high clouds of fine spray that drifted across the road. Emma pulled the window closed and shivered. She could smell bacon and guessed that Tim was already downstairs preparing breakfast.

Slowly she dressed and went to join him.

One more day together after this. That's all.

Her gaze followed him as he moved round the kitchen, studying his face, his hair, his long lean body, every gesture, every movement, impressing them on her memory to keep for ever.

She drank her coffee without tasting it. Crumbled her toast into fragments on the plate. Desperately wishing they were in one of the sunny coves together, not surrounded by the violence of a storm.

Tim went across to the window and stared through it. 'Doesn't look as though it's going to get better, but we could drive over to Falmouth. Visit the Maritime Museum, maybe. At least we'd be out of the wind in there. What do you think? Or would you rather go home today instead?'

'No!' Emma didn't want their remaining time together to end so soon. 'Let's go to Falmouth.'

*　　*　　*

She followed Tim round each floor of the museum, not even noticing the boats or displays. Only wanting to be with him. Near him. The day seemed to be going too fast. Surrounded by chattering people and excited, shrieking children, they sat in the cafeteria, looking out at the harbour where huge ships were moored for repair, or waiting, ready to put to sea once more.

'Emma!' Alison's voice made her jump. 'Fancy seeing you here, of all places. How are you now?' She swung forward the baby held on her hip. 'And this is Charlotte. Don't you think she's beautiful?'

Startled by their unexpected meeting, Emma stared in confusion at the chubby baby, chewing a biscuit, before glancing quickly round to see whether Steve was there too.

Alison turned to Tim. 'You're Emma's

gorgeous boyfriend, aren't you? Remember me? I was in hospital with her.' Without waiting for an answer, she chattered on. 'Steve's taken Mark down to watch the waves. He was getting a bit bored in here. Likes boats, but not so many all at once. Look, you can see them through the window down there. We've just bought Mark that red anorak and he's so excited.' She leaned closer to the glass looking anxious. 'I do hope Steve's got a tight hold on Mark's hand. He's getting so venturesome and keeps running off.' She turned to Emma. 'Now, tell me what you've been up to since you left hospital. You look really tanned.'

'Can I get you a coffee or something, Alison?' Tim pushed back his chair and stood up. 'And the little girl?'

'Ooh, thanks. That's kind of you. Just a cup of milk for Charlie and I'll have a cappuccino, if that's all right?'

Tim was carrying the tray to the table when there was a sudden sound of shouting outside. Emma went to the window, and looked down.

A small child, in a bright red anorak with the hood pulled up over its head, was scampering to where waves hurtled against the sea wall, sending spray crashing down onto the path. A fair-haired man followed, calling out to the little boy to stop.

Emma held her breath, her chest tightening as she watched.

The man was Steve. And the child could

only be his little son, Mark.

Others were running towards them now, their voices carried by the wind as they, too, cried out a warning. Abruptly, the little boy stopped running and started to turn as, from behind him, a torrent of water rose high into the air, cascading down over the path—and the child was gone.

Steve's yell of anguish reached up to her in the restaurant as he dived straight into the boiling sea. Pressing her face closer to the glass, Emma saw two men jump in after him, watched them flung sideways by the next surge of water. Others crouched on the wet stone, bending dangerously forward.

Turning her head, Emma realised that Alison was standing rigid as a statue beside her, face drained of any colour, whispering the same words over and over again. 'Oh, no! Please, no!'

The wail of a siren echoed, growing in volume as it came nearer. Silence filled the restaurant. People lined the windows, staring down. Faces horrified. Arms tightly clutching their own small children. Everyone helpless. All they could do was watch the tragedy taking place in front of them.

Charlotte started to wail. Automatically, Alison put a biscuit into her waiting hand.

Overhead a helicopter clattered, swooping in low over the waves as it began to make a series of circles. A gasp went up from those watching as someone dropped through its open door to snake down, twisting round and round on the cable, buffeted by the wind, before being hidden from their vision in a mist of spray.

When it cleared, the helicopter was hovering, the roar of its engine vibrating the whole museum. Emma thought she could see a red bundle, clutched against the crewman's body, disappear in through its doorway.

'Oh, Tim, this is terrible,' she murmured, before realising he wasn't there.

Frantically, she looked out through the window, staring down to where dark shapes were gathered, drenched by those overpowering waves, Was Tim one of them? Had his natural instinct been to help? Was saving lives part of his training too?

An ambulance, led by a police car, hurtled across, blue lights flashing, siren shrieking. A couple of paramedics ran to where a group of people crouched round something on the ground.

Emma closed her eyes, fighting against the faintness that was threatening to overcome her. A cold hand touched her wrist and she opened them again, her breath sighing out in relief when she saw Tim, drenched by seawater. But his stricken expression told her what he was going to say.

Gently, he put an arm round Alison and guided her to a chair.

'Steve was so brave, Alison. He fought desperately to reach Mark. And he almost succeeded, but finally the force of the waves was too strong and dragged him down.' He took both her hands. 'They're searching for him.'

'And Mark?' Alison whispered, her eyes drowned by tears.

'He'll be fine. The helicopter is on its way to the hospital with him. I'll take you there now.'

'But Charlie . . . ' Alison held the bewildered baby close to her cheek.

'You'll stay with her, won't you, Emma, until Alison's aunt arrives? Someone's been sent to collect her.'

* * *

'Alison doesn't have to know about Steve, does she, Tim?' Emma pleaded, late that afternoon, when they drove back to Coverack. 'He'll always be a hero in her eyes for trying to save little Mark— and losing his own life by doing so. Can't it stay that way?'

Tim's fingers brushed lightly across the back of her hand. 'It's really up to you. If that's how you want it to be.'

'That's how I want it to be,' she replied.

* * *

Now it really was their last day in Cornwall. A

126

day that dawned with an amazing brightness that so often follows stormy weather. With everything packed into her rucksack, Emma gazed out to where the sea glinted beyond the tiny harbour and fishing boats swung lazily from their anchor chains.

If only it had been like this yesterday, Emma thought, *Steve would still be alive and with his family.* Fate, though, had changed all that.

'There's a little beach near here,' Tim said, putting his coffee mug into the sink after they'd finished breakfast. 'Just the right place to remember once we're home again. I think you'll like it.'

A while later she was gazing out of the car window at soft yellow sand and shingle, surrounded by tumbled granite rocks, and an unruffled blue sea stretching away into the distance, where a little church was tucked into the dunes, almost on the beach.

'Here we are. So what do you think?' Tim asked, stopping the car.

'Peaceful. Quiet. Secluded. Just how I like it,' she answered contentedly.

'How about—romantic?'

Emma looked across at him in surprise before, with one hand cupping her chin, his mouth closed over hers.

'Are policemen allowed to kiss their . . . what do you call us when we're not criminals?' she asked, quite a long time afterwards.

'We're not like doctors and their patients,

Emma,' he murmured huskily, kissing her again.

'So I'm realising.'

Tim leaned away from her. 'Can you ever forgive that it was my fault you lost your baby?'

'Of course it wasn't! We could have been killed, if you hadn't swerved onto the verge.' Emma put her hands over his. 'Everything that's happened has been by chance. I wasn't meant to have Steve's child. If I had done, no matter how much I loved the baby, he or she would always have been Steve's child. I'd never have been able to forget him. And I need to do that. To start my life again.'

Tim reached up to push back the sunroof of the car, letting in warmth and soft salt air. 'Would you consider starting it again with me, Emma?' He hesitated and looked down. 'I know it's much too soon to ask you, remembering how much you loved Steve.'

'Once,' she answered slowly, 'I did love him very much, but I was over Steve quite a while ago—the day I fell in love with you, Tim.' Emma lowered her gaze. 'There's something I have to confess, though.'

He sighed in mock exasperation. 'More withholding evidence from the police, Emma?' He smiled and his eyes crinkled at the corners in the way she'd grown to love. 'Like not telling me that the woman in hospital with you was Steve's wife? Or that it was Steve who was driving the red car that ran us off the road?'

She stared back at him. 'You *knew*?'

'Yes, Emma, I knew. I passed Steve Jones in the corridor the first day I came to see you at the hospital.'

'And you didn't arrest him?'

'I had far more important things on my mind that day. You, Emma. There was no way I was going to stop and make an arrest. All I wanted was to be with you. I always will.' He stroked one finger along the curve of her lips. 'So, what do you want to confess? Or is it going to take the bright lights and a diet of bread and water for me to get at the truth?'

'A cream tea might do it.'

'With strawberry jam? That's a promise. So come on, then, reveal this terrible confession.'

Her fingers tightened round his as she said in a rush, 'Steve gave me back the fifty thousand pounds.'

'Oh, no!' Bemused, Emma took in the horrified expression in Tim's eyes. 'Can't you give it away, or something?'

'Why on earth would I want to do that?'

'You'll think I'm only marrying you for your money.'

She laughed. 'You did ask me before you even knew I'd got it all back.'

He slipped his fingers away from hers and drew her closer. 'Well, thank goodness for that! Now—can I continue where I left off, before you interrupted me?'

'You mean, about the cream tea?' Emma

teased, lifting her face to his.

'No, about this,' he murmured, letting his lips give the answer.

As he kissed her, she remembered the words of her grandmother's bequest—*To my beloved granddaughter Emma Louise, that she may find everlasting happiness.*

And now Emma knew that, finally, her wish was going to come true.

Chivers Large Print Direct

If you have enjoyed this Large Print book and would like to build up your own collection of Large Print books and have them delivered direct to your door, please contact **Chivers Large Print Direct**.

Chivers Large Print Direct offers you a full service:

- ≤ **Created to support your local library**
- ≤ **Delivery direct to your door**
- ≤ **Easy-to-read type and attractively bound**
- ≤ **The very best authors**
- ≤ **Special low prices**

For further details either call Customer Services on 01225 443400 or write to us at

Chivers Large Print Direct
FREEPOST (BA 1686/1)
Bath
BA1 3QZ